TEXAS
Wesleyan
UNIVERSITY

THE EUNICE AND JAMES L. WEST LIBRARY

GIFT OF

the School of Library and
Information Studies, Texas Woman's
University

NOTHING BUT TROUBLE, TROUBLE, TROUBLE

NOTHING BUT TROUBLE, TROUBLE, TROUBLE

PATRICIA HERMES

SCHOLASTIC HARDCOVER

Scholastic Inc.
New York

Library of Congress Cataloging-in-Publication Data

Hermes, Patricia.
Nothing but trouble, trouble, trouble / by Patricia Hermes.
p.   cm.
Summary: To prove to her parents that she is grown up enough to
babysit, Alex tries to stay out of trouble for two weeks.

ISBN 0-590-43499-3

[1. Behavior—Fiction. 2. Growth—Fiction.]   I. Title.
PZ7.H4317Nr   1994
[Fic]—dc20   93-13968
                                                          CIP
                                                          AC

12 11 10 9 8 7 6 5 4 3 2 1   4 5 6 7 8/9

Printed in the U.S.A.   37

First Scholastic printing, March 1994

NOTHING BUT TROUBLE, TROUBLE, TROUBLE

One

I knew I shouldn't laugh. I was in enough trouble already. But it was awfully hard not to.

Dad told me, when he saw me outside in the pouring rain before he called this boring family conference, "Alexandra Warner, this is no laughing matter. We trusted you to take care of Meg! There's nothing funny about this."

And so here we all were gathered around the kitchen table. Mom and Dad were sitting next to each other, both of them still wearing their office clothes, and Daddy hadn't even taken off his raincoat. They were also wearing those superserious looks they get at these family conferences. My brother, Mark, Mr. Perfect, was slouched in a chair, looking bored. And I was standing at the end of the table with my

1

little sister, Meg. I kept darting looks at her, trying not to laugh.

I really did know I was in big trouble. Whenever Dad calls me by my full name, I know it's serious. Still, every time I snuck a look at Meg, I could feel this laugh bubbling up. She was covered with mud, and I mean covered. I was pretty muddy, too, my feet *skushing* it inside my shoes, but nothing like Meg. She was caked with the stuff, top to toe. The only thing not completely covered were her pigtails, and they were so dirty and stiff they practically stuck straight out.

And that's when it struck me: a Popsicle! Meg looked just like one of those chocolate-covered twin Popsicles. As soon as that thought hit me, I did laugh.

I threw a hand over my mouth, but it was too late. The laugh had already escaped.

Both Mom and Dad glared at me.

"I'm sorry! I'm sorry!" I said, holding up my hand. "I know it's not funny. I know I made a mistake. It's just that I had this thought."

"You always have a thought," Mom said with a sigh. "Only problem is, not when you should."

"I know," I said. And that was probably true. "It's just that Meg looks just like a chocolate-covered Popsicle."

Mark made a sudden bleating little sound and then put both hands over his mouth and began coughing.

I didn't dare look at him.

Neither Mom nor Dad looked like they thought it was funny, though.

Neither did Meg. She turned to me, her lower lip thrust out, looking supermad. "That's not nice, Alex," she said.

I moved closer to her, my feet going *skush, skush* on the tile floor. "I'm sorry, Meg," I said. "I'm not laughing *at* you, honest." I held out one filthy hand. "Look, I'm almost as bad as you." I patted her stiff hair.

I turned to Mom and Dad then. "Can I go get cleaned up now?" I asked. "I'll give Meg a bath, too."

"In a minute," Dad said. "I want to get something clear first. Again — once more — I want to hear how this happened. Why were you and Meg out in the pouring rain, and how did you get to look the way you look? I want the whole story. And I want to know *why,* too."

He said it in his most lawyerlike voice, and I wondered for the zillionth time how come I had to be stuck with a dad who's a lawyer. Most of the time, he's a nice dad. And when he isn't horrified with me for something I've done, we're good friends. I know a lot of girls who wish they had a dad as nice as mine. But when he puts on his lawyer act, he's really a pain.

I started to speak, but Mark interrupted. "Can I go now?" he asked, standing up. "I wasn't in on this and I have a science project due tomorrow. Want me to start supper?"

"Yes, yes, that would be nice," Mom said. "We'll be with you in a minute."

I watched while Mr. Perfect went to the refrigerator and started taking things out.

I wouldn't have thought to offer to make dinner. How did he even know where to begin? It must be nice to be as perfect as he is — to never get in trouble, to be so responsible. And me, I was in trouble just because I was trying to be grown-up in the first place!

I sighed and turned back to Mom and Dad.

"Okay, Alex," Dad said, shrugging his arms out of his raincoat. "Go on. Let's hear it. *What* happened? And *why*?"

I slipped an arm around Meg and pulled her closer. "It happened," I said, "because I want to be allowed to baby-sit. Not just for two hours on Friday for Meg, but for nighttimes, for other kids. For pay! You won't let me, but everybody else in class is allowed. They're earning tons of money, and I need money. Everybody else has had their ears pierced, even Elizabeth and — "

"Alex!" Dad interrupted. "Alex, what does this have to do with my question?"

"I'm trying to tell you," I said. "Just listen. All the way through, okay?"

"Okay," Dad said.

"We're listening," Mom said.

"Okay," I said. "Today is Friday, right?"

Dad rolled his eyes, but he didn't interrupt.

"Friday," I went on, "is the one day Meg isn't in day care after school, right?"

This time Mom rolled her eyes, but she just nodded.

"Okay," I said. "On Friday, I take care of Meg for two hours. I'm just supposed to stay in the house with her, right? But at school today, Mr. Griffin, our science teacher, he said that next week we're going to be doing a new project —

a project that will teach us to be responsible. We have to take care of a pet for a whole week-end or else we have to carry around an egg — like, *all the time,* the whole weekend — pre-tending we're its mother. And Elizabeth and I were talking about how dumb that was, how much more responsible it was to baby-sit than egg-sit. And Elizabeth found out in her baby-sitting course — 'cause, like I said, she's al-lowed to sit, just like everyone else — she learned that you're not supposed to just *sit* the kids; you're supposed to *entertain* them! So I decided to show you I can entertain Meg, like a good sitter, and then maybe you'd let me baby-sit. For money. For *real* kids. Well, I mean, I know Meg is real, but you know what I mean. And for real money. So I decided to entertain her by getting her a video and — "

"Beauty and the Beast," Meg interrupted. "She was going to get me *Beauty and the Beast.* But it was my money."

"Well," I said. "I don't have any, which is one of the problems. So anyway, we went to the video store — "

"By way of a mud slide?" Mom asked. She pushed wearily at her hair, pushing it out of her face. Mom's a social worker for little kids and orphan babies mostly. She works hard, trying to find homes for them when something happens to their families, and I wondered if she'd had a hard day.

"We didn't mean for that to happen," I said. "We just took a shortcut through the back alley by Robin's place, and they were doing this construction, I think digging a swimming pool for next summer."

"You were in a construction site?" Mom asked.

"Someone else's private property?" Dad asked.

"Not exactly in it!" I said. "It was sort of next to it. They had scooped up some dirt and left it in a pile, like a really neat hill and this plastic bag was lying there — "

"And Alex said it would make a good sled, and it did!" Meg interrupted, her eyes shining.

"But after just one slide, with the rain and all, we were pretty dirty," I said.

"Yucky," Meg said.

"So we figured we might as well keep right on sliding," I said. "Then when we were finished, we came home to take a bath, and that's when you caught us — I mean, saw us."

"Alex," Mom said quietly, shaking her head

slowly back and forth. "Alex, let me be sure I
understand something. Your idea was to prove
that you could baby-sit?"

"Right," I said. "That I was grown-up."

I heard Mark make that little bleating sound
again, and I sent him a dirty look.

"Well," Dad said. "I'm afraid you have a ways
to go to prove responsibility to me. In fact, I
think perhaps Meg shouldn't be left in your
care for even those two hours! I think we
should put her back in day care Fridays."

"No!" Meg said, clinging to me. "Jeff comes
to day care Fridays and he beats me up. Alex
is a good sitter!"

"I don't know," Dad said, standing up. "I'm
afraid Alex was very careless today."

Dad looked at me. "You know Meg is very
susceptible to colds, Alex. Yet you played in a
mud hill. In the rain. On a cold day. At a construction site. On someone else's private property. Not a crime, certainly, but surely a . . .
misdemeanor." He paused and actually smiled
when he said that. "And you make Meg an
accessory. I can't see how that's responsible."

"Lawyer talk!" I said. "And you're wrong. I
am responsible enough. I'll show you."

"I wish you would," Dad said.

"I'll second that!" Mom said. And she had that weary sound in her voice again. "I certainly wish you could show us that."

"Well, I will!" I said. "You'll see."

"How?" Dad asked.

"How?" I repeated.

"Yes, how?" Dad asked. "How will you show us you're responsible?"

"Easy!" I said.

Mom and Dad were both looking at me.

I saw Mark stop what he was doing at the stove, and even he turned around and looked at me.

How? How could I prove it? *Why* should I prove it?

To baby-sit. To get money. To have my ears pierced.

I folded my arms and tried for a lawyer-type voice, just like Dad's.

"Okay," I said. "How about this? This responsibility project for science class I was telling you about, caring for an egg or a pet for a whole weekend — "

"No pets in this house!" Mom interrupted. "You know Meg's allergic."

"An egg, then!" I said. "If I get an A in that project, carrying around a stupid egg every minute of that whole, entire weekend, that will prove it, won't it? Prove that I'm responsible?"

I saw Mom and Dad exchange a look.

Mom bent close and said something to Dad. Dad nodded and looked at me.

"Tell you what," Dad said. "If you get an A in that science project — *and* an A from us here at home — we'll reconsider about the baby-sitting."

"What do you mean, an A from you?" I asked.

"Just that you show more responsibility at home, especially with Meg," Mom said. "That you don't get yourself — or her — in trouble. That you're a good example for her."

"A good sample?" Meg said.

"EX-ample," I said.

"So what do you say?" Dad said.

"For how long?" I asked.

"A month?" Mom said.

"A *month*?" I said. "No way! The science project is just a weekend!"

"You can do it for a month," Mom said. "I know you can."

She stood up then and came over to me. I

saw her reach out like she was going to put an arm around me, but then she backed away.

I didn't blame her. I really was very disgustingly muddy.

"I know you don't mean to get in trouble," Mom said, leaning over and kissing me lightly, right in the middle of my forehead. "You're not a bad kid — you're a very, very good one, a wonderful child. But you have to learn to be less — less impulsive or something."

"Right," Dad said. "So what do you say? Is it a deal? An A in the school project, an A at home, and we reconsider the baby-sitting ban."

"You're asking a lot," I said.

They both just smiled.

"You can do it!" Meg whispered, leaning against me and looking up at me. "You're a good sample. Say, yes."

"How about two weeks?" I asked.

"Three," Dad said.

"Two," I repeated.

Mom laughed right out loud. "All right, two weeks!" she said. "I'll go for that."

She turned to Dad. "Two uneventful weeks would be spectacular," she said.

"It's a deal," I said. "You wait and see."

"Yea!" Meg whispered to me.

She slipped her hand into mine then and I led her up to the bathroom. To start the new project.

Baby-sitting. Money!

A lot was riding on the next two weeks.

Two

If a really lot was riding on these next two weeks, why was I doing what I was doing — standing in the alley by Robin's house on the following Friday after school, with Robin's two cats in pillowcases, one dangling from each hand? I was only borrowing the cats — *borrowing* them — because this was the weekend for the responsibility project, and I had to get an A. And there was no way I was going to baby-sit an egg all weekend! Yet I knew I was taking a really big risk. I mean, Robin was away for the weekend, so she'd never know I'd taken the cats. But if anything happened to them, I'd be in big trouble. And even if nothing happened, if Mom or Dad found out, I was in *big, big, big* trouble.

Still, nobody would know. Nobody. Not if I

could help it. Just Meg and Elizabeth — and I needed them both in this project.

I looked at Meg now. "If we drop them, we're dead," I whispered to her.

"I'm not dropping them!" Meg whispered back. "I'm not touching them!"

She held her hands behind her back, and even though it was nearly five o'clock and already kind of dark in the alley, still I could see that stubborn look on her face that she gets so often.

"Please?" I said. "Take one? They're very fat cats. They're heavy."

But Meg shook her head, her blonde pigtails swinging from side to side so hard that they slapped her in the face. "No, Alex," she said. "I'll get in trouble. I told you, I'm just the lookout."

"Lookouts could at least help carry!" I said.

I set the cats down for a minute, but held tight to the top of the pillowcases. I suddenly saw claws jab out through one of the pillowcases, then disappear.

"I can't!" Meg said. "Remember how Daddy said last week that I'm an ex . . . ax . . . excess . . ."

"An accessory!" I muttered.

"That's what I said," she said. "I'm a next cessory if you do something bad and I help. I don't want to be in trouble, too, like that other time."

I didn't know if she just meant last week in the mud or some different time, but it didn't matter much. There were plenty of other times, I knew. Things were going to be different now, though, now that I had made that deal — I'd be a good example for Meg, and get that A at school, or die trying.

Yet here I was with two kidnapped cats! I sighed.

Still, it would be all right. No one would find out. And it was the best way I knew to get the A.

I shifted the pillowcases from one arm to the other. The cats were very heavy, and wiggly, too, throwing me off-balance. Thank goodness they weren't meowing anymore, though. We were still much too close to Robin's yard. When we had first snuck into her yard and into the garage, it had been surprisingly easy to slide the cats into the pillowcases. Once I picked them up, I just slipped the pillowcases over their heads. It was only *after* they were in that it was a problem, with them yowling like crazy.

"Yeah, well," I said, "if we get caught, we're *both* in big trouble, accessory or not."

"Not me!" Meg said, and I could see the scared look on her face. "I'm not helping. I told you I'm just lookout."

I decided it was kinder not to tell her that lookouts could be accessories to a crime, too. That was one of the big problems with having a father who was a lawyer. You got to know stuff you didn't want to know. And I did feel bad about getting Meg in on a trick like this after promising to be a good example for her.

But was it only a trick? Or was stealing two cats worse, a felony maybe?

A felony is really bad. Grown-ups go to jail for it. They don't send kids to jail, but they do write it down and then you have a record. That's a little like your permanent record at school, only worse.

"Don't worry," I said. "We won't get caught. And you're not in trouble. But go look now. Be sure nobody's coming."

Meg raced to the end of the long, narrow alley that runs along the back of Robin's garage, separating it from the church next door.

"It's safe!" Meg called, peering out from the end of the alley. "Nobody out there!"

Great! Yell it!

I tiptoed to the end of the alley, holding one pillowcase in each hand.

I stopped and looked out myself once more, just to be sure the coast was clear.

Okay.

I took a deep breath. And made a dash for it. Racing. Across the street. Around the corner and halfway up the block to our house. Across the back lawn. To the garage that's at the back of our property. And into the side garage door.

I could hear Meg racing along behind me, and in a minute she slid in the door, too.

There! Safe!

"We did it, Alex!" Meg said. Her eyes were shining. "We did it! And nobody saw us!"

Us? I guess she had forgotten about being an accessory.

I set the pillowcases down on the floor very gently.

One bag — one cat — had begun meowing and thrashing about like crazy again, but there was no sound at all from the other bag. It was silent. And absolutely still.

Oh, man, what if I'd killed one of them? That would really be a felony, wouldn't it? Robin is always bragging about how much everything costs, and I knew these were Himalayan cats, so they were probably really expensive. Robin doesn't have anything that isn't expensive. One day at school she actually added up how much the clothes cost that she was wearing that day, and it came to more than five hundred dollars! At least, that's what she said. I bet anything these cats were superexpensive, too, purebred or pure gold or pure something. And if you steal — or even borrow — something expensive, it's worse than if you steal something cheap.

I looked at the two bags, one meowing, one quiet.

"You untie that bag," I said to Meg, nodding my head at the quiet bag. "I'll do this one. I'm afraid this'll scratch you."

"Okay," Meg said cheerfully.

Weird how one five-year-old sister can make you feel like a mean rat. But I didn't take the offer back.

I untied the string around my pillowcase. I wasn't taking any chances on getting scratched so when I untied it, I stepped back, fast.

Robin's cat Tootsie — or maybe it was Mootsie because they both look exactly alike, all white and fluffy — came streaking out of the bag, her fur sticking up in every direction. She leapt from the floor onto the windowsill, then up onto Dad's workbench. There, she gathered herself together and launched herself onto a rafter. She sat there glaring down at us, looking just like a Halloween cat, except that she was the wrong color.

Behind me, there was still no sound from the other bag.

"How's Mootsie? Or Tootsie?" I asked, still without looking.

"He's asleep," Meg said. She was whispering. "I think he's tired."

Oh, boy.

"Asleep?" I repeated, still without turning around.

"Uh-huh," she whispered. "You were right. Putting them in pillowcases makes them sleepy. He's cute."

Cute? Or dead?

I had to turn around and look. Mom is always telling me I should be more careful of Meg, that she's a very "sensitive" child and I should stop traumatizing her. It wasn't fair to Meg to let her sit there patting a dead cat.

Actually, Meg shouldn't be touching any cat, dead or alive, because like Mom said, Meg's so allergic. But then, it was partly Meg's fault that I had to borrow these cats since we can't have our own pet because of her allergies.

I took a deep breath and turned around.

Meg was sitting cross-legged on the floor, the pillowcase open, the cat curled up inside it, sleeping. Or dead.

I came closer.

Meg was stroking the cat, patting its head over and over, as gently as if she were a real mom with a real live baby.

I bent closer.

Purring! The cat was purring. It wasn't dead!

And just then Meg sneezed.

"Uh-oh," I said. "You'd better leave him alone."

"It's okay," Meg said. "He likes me."

Actually, what she said was, "Idth oday. He lied ne."

I looked at her. Her eyes were already red-rimmed and puffy-looking, and a red flush was spreading up her neck.

"Meg!" I pulled her hand away and Mootsie or Tootsie stood up and stretched. "Don't touch him anymore," I said. "You'll get sick."

"I don't get sick," she said. "I get allergy."
She rubbed her eyes.

"Same thing!" I said. I grabbed her hand and
held it tightly, keeping it away from her eyes.
"Let's go inside and wash your hands and get
the cat fuzz off."

She sneezed again and pulled away from me.
"But who's going to take care of them?" she
said. She sounded like she was going to cry.
"They'll be lonely."

"*I'm* taking care of them and they won't be
lonely!" I said. "I told you I'd take care of
them — and I will, *good* care of them. I'd never
hurt a cat."

"But you *stole* them!" she said.

"*Borrowed* them," I said.

"But how come?" she asked.

I took her by the hand, led her to the garage
door and outside, then closed the door tightly.

"Come on," I said. "If Mom sees you like this,
she'll find out what happened and then —
trouble! Besides, you know why I took them,
you were there that last Friday — I need an A
in the science project."

"And an A about me," Meg added virtuously.

"Right," I said.

I started leading her across the back lawn to the house.

Actually, even though she knew about the baby-sitting, she didn't really know why I wanted the money.

I had to save for two things. The most important is having my ears pierced. *Everybody* in class has had theirs done already, except me. When I got some money, I'd do it right away, although I wasn't going to tell Mom till it was over. She didn't say I couldn't — just said she wouldn't pay for it. She says it's foolish to mutilate your body that way. Ha! She doesn't have to listen to Robin say anyone who hasn't had hers done yet was a baby. Anyway, I was going to do it, but I hadn't figured out yet who could go with me. You have to have an adult. But I'd figure that out, too. Maybe one of Elizabeth's big sisters. And when I earned more money, I was going to buy a Barbie's dream house. It's dumb, I know, and I'd never tell anyone, not even Elizabeth, my best friend, because only little kids want a Barbie's dream house. But I've wanted one for years, and Mom and Dad won't buy me TV toys. So I'd buy one for myself.

"But why cats?" Meg asked now.

"Cats? I told you," I said. "Mr. Griffin gave us our choice of responsibility assignments, and we have to do it *all* weekend! We have to care for a real pet, feeding it, holding it, and everything. We have to document all the time we spend on it. We're on our honor to do it. That, or else we have to carry around an egg all weekend, starting at nine tomorrow morning, pretending we're its mother! We can't put it down, or leave it alone unless we get a baby-sitter for it — can you believe that? We have to act like a mother hen! What would you do if you had a choice like that?"

"Steal two cats like you did," she said very seriously. "But what if Robin finds out?"

"Will you stop saying that?" I said. "I didn't *steal* them! I borrowed them. Besides, the Popularity Princess won't find out because she's going to be away all weekend. She's going to care for her horse, she told Mr. Griffin. She keeps it at her family's horse farm in the country. All she talks about is horses. You know what, Meg? I think Robin is part horse herself."

"Really?" Meg said.

I just rolled my eyes. Five-year-olds have no sense of humor at all.

I took Meg into the house and into the kitchen. I knew Mom wasn't home because she always does the grocery shopping after work on Friday afternoons. I also knew it was too early for Dad to be home from work yet. And I was pretty sure Mark wouldn't be home, either, because on Friday he has soccer.

Mark's really great at soccer, as well as practically everything else. He's a computer whiz, a baseball star, a basketball star, an all-state soccer star, an Eagle Scout. He's even an honor student.

And he offers to make dinner without being told! Geez!

Besides all that, he's gorgeous. At least, that's what all my friends think, Robin especially. She scribbles his name all over her notebooks and is always trying to get me to bring him to parties and stuff.

Actually, he's pretty nice to have as a brother. I mean, I like him, and most people I know hate their big brothers. Well, most of the time I like him, when he's not being too disgustingly wonderful.

I wonder sometimes, though, if it's hard being as wonderful as he is. Me, I'll never have to worry about that! Although secretly, I do wish sometimes that Mom and Dad would think I was wonderful, too. Especially last week, when I saw how upset they were. I think that's at least part of why I made that deal, not just for the money, but to show them.

When we got in the kitchen, Meg climbed up on the step stool at the sink. Even on the stool, she couldn't reach the faucet, so I turned it on for her and helped her wash her hands. Then I made her bend down and stick her head under the faucet so the cold water could run on her face for a while, and get the cat fuzz and dander washed off.

She's such a patient little kid, letting me do that.

Just then, the phone rang and I grabbed it.

It was Elizabeth. Elizabeth talks nonstop. Fast. And loud. It's as if everything she says is in capital letters. I think maybe it's because she has six sisters and that's the only way to get attention in her house. But she's my best friend and has been since kindergarten. We do practically everything together. She had even been going to help with the catnapping, but at lunchtime some rubber bands broke on her braces and she had to go home early to go to the orthodontist.

To be honest, I had been a little relieved. I was afraid that she wouldn't be able to be quiet long enough to sneak over Robin's huge privacy fence and into the garage to snatch the cats.

"Are you going?" That's the first thing she said when I picked up the phone, not even saying hello. "What are you wearing? Should we dress alike? Are you going? Should we pick you up?"

"Going where?" I asked.

"Robin's!" She sounded impatient. "Didn't she call you? Sure she did. She invited everybody in class, I mean, all the girls, for a sleepover. Her mom was supposed to take her to that farm for the weekend, remember, the horse farm? But then they couldn't go, something about her dad's work, so her mom's making it up to her by letting her have this huge sleepover and it's tonight and everybody's going. She didn't call?" She finally paused for breath.

Tonight! Robin wasn't going to her horse farm. If she wasn't caring for her horse, she'd want her cats.

Cats that were in *my* garage!

I looked down at the phone. The little light on the answering machine was blinking.

"Hold on a minute," I said slowly. "There's a message on the machine. I was outside."

I pushed the button and listened: "Hi, Alex, this is Robin!" the voice said. "I'm having a sleep-over tonight. Can you come? It's at seven-thirty and everybody's coming, so call me back."

I reset the machine and swallowed hard. "Elizabeth?" I said weakly into the phone. "The cats!"

"What about them?"

"You know what about them."

"You didn't *do* it?" Elizabeth yelled. "But she *called.* She's not going away. She's staying here. Her mom is letting her have a sleepover 'cause they didn't go away, and the sleepover's in just an hour, well, maybe more but . . . *Why did you do that*?"

"Maybe the sleepover's tomorrow night?" I said, even though I knew that was ridiculous, that I had just heard her say "tonight" on the machine. And I was dead.

"Of course I'm sure!" Elizabeth said. Her voice was rising. "You did that really? But she *called.* She called everyone, she even — "

"I'm freezing!" Meg yelled. "I'm dripping! I need a towel!"

"Elizabeth?" I said. "I got to go! I got to get the cats back!"

"Alex Warner," Elizabeth said. "You are in big trouble. Big, big, big, big, *big trouble.*"

I surely was.

Beside me, Meg had scrambled off the step stool, yelling and dripping and shivering and she'd probably end up in the hospital with an allergy attack or with pneumonia. Some good example I was!

I was beginning to have a feeling that this cat thing was turning out to be a whole lot worse than just a felony.

Three

I dried Meg, then whisked her upstairs. We made a deal: She'd tell Mom her allergies came because she ate something she wasn't supposed to eat. And I'd let her borrow my two favorite things — my entire Barbie collection that I've been gathering since I was four, and my very own little TV that I got as a combination Christmas and birthday present last year, the thing I'd wanted more than anything in the world so far. And I was letting her have both in her room for three entire days!

I thought that was totally unfair, but Meg said it was a bargain. She originally wanted a whole week. So what else could I do but agree? Her face was still really red and her eyes were still very puffy and if Mom and Dad knew how come, I'd be in big trouble. I guess I mean bigger trouble.

Meg is allergic to lots of things besides cats — strawberries and chocolate and tomatoes and wheat and eggs and whey. I don't even know what whey is exactly but it's something to do with milk or cheese and Meg's very allergic to it. When she gets one of her really bad allergy attacks, all she can eat is tuna fish (if it's packed in water), rice, and rice cakes. Rice cakes taste exactly like lined white notebook paper. I know. I used to eat notebook paper when I was a kid.

Meg is also allergic to telling lies. Her face gets bright red when she does. But her face was already so red that Mom wouldn't know the difference. Anyway, Meg promised she'd tell Mom she had eaten an Oreo.

As soon as I saw that Meg was really all right, not wheezing or anything, I took off for the garage to capture the cats. I got the last cans of tuna from the kitchen cabinet and took them with me to help coax the cats into the pillowcases again. I had a plan: After I captured them, I'd just dump them over that big privacy fence that surrounds Robin's yard and the garage. I wouldn't try to put them back *in* the garage, because to do that I'd have to climb over the fence and into the yard myself. Better to just dump them over the fence and pray that Robin thought the garage door had just swung open by itself.

But when I got out to our garage, both Mootsie and Tootsie were perched atop a rafter, side by side, glaring down at me. And nothing I could do — nothing, not even the tuna fish — would persuade them to come down. For an entire hour, I chased those cats. An hour!

It was now after six o'clock. The sleepover was at seven-thirty! I had to get those cats back. I was already a week into this deal — a week of showing how grown-up I was. I couldn't screw this up now.

And what could be more screwed up than losing Robin's solid-gold cats?

I climbed up on Dad's workbench and tried setting a can of tuna up on the rafter. But both cats just ambled to the other end — and if Dad knew I was on his precious workbench, I'd be in even bigger trouble, especially as I was tiptoeing over his newest masterpiece, a rocking horse he had just made for Mom's office.

Next, I got a ladder and put it up at the far end of the rafter where the cats had gone, then

I put another opened can of tuna fish there.

"Please, Mootsie! Please, Tootsie!" I whispered. "Robin will kill me!"

But as soon as they saw me, they retreated somewhere else. And then, both stupid cats began to act like they were enjoying the chase. They began zooming from rafter to rafter to rafter as if they were birds or bats. One of them was even smiling, its teeth showing and its lips pulled back, in an idiot kind of grin.

"Stupid cats!" I shouted at them. "Why don't you *act* like cats?"

One of them hissed at me.

I hissed back.

"Okay," I said. "Get serious. I *need* to return you to your home. No more fooling around. I'll be in big trouble. Mom and Dad will get called to Robin's, or even to the police station! Don't you know you're very expensive cats?"

They just grinned some more.

I looked at my watch.

Six-fifteen. Suppertime. Mom would be home and Dad, too. And probably by now, Robin had discovered that her cats were missing and her mom had maybe even called the police and Elizabeth was coming in just an hour! Not only that, but what was I going to do about the science project once I put the cats back? I'd have to care for a stupid egg!

I looked up at the cats once more. They were now on the back rafter, and all I could see was two tails hanging down.

Two tails. I was tempted. But I didn't.

I'd come back here and try again after dinner.

I started back to the house but first I made sure to close the garage door tightly. The worst thing I could do would be to lose the cats completely.

Mom and Dad were in the kitchen making dinner when I came in, and Mark was there, too. Mark was telling Dad how much he liked Dad's latest woodworking project, that rocking horse for Mom's clients. Some of the kids Mom works with are poor and have no toys, so she needs toys to keep in her office. Dad loves making them for her. He's always out at his workbench in the garage. Fortunately, though, he mostly just works there on Sundays, and I would surely have the cats out of there by then.

Mark was also setting the table while he talked — setting the table and it was *my* turn!

Geez!

"Hi, honey," Mom said when I came in.

"Where have you been? It's dark out already."

"Just out," I said.

"Hi, Alex!" Dad said, smiling at me. "I thought you were upstairs in your room. I heard your TV going." He came and gave me a big hug.

I hugged him back, and looked up at him. I was glad we were friends again.

I pulled away then and went over to the sink to wash the tuna fish stink off my hands.

"I was putting my bike away," I said.

"Since when?" Mark said, but he was laughing.

"I can be responsible, too!" I said back. "You're not the only one who's Mr. Wonderful." I made a face at him.

He shrugged. "What's the matter with you?" he asked.

I ignored him. "Mom?" I said. "Can I go to a sleepover at Robin's tonight?"

"I thought you didn't like Robin," Mom said.

"I hate her," I said.

"Makes sense," Mark said.

I glared at him.

He laughed. "You know what?" he said. "Some girl keeps calling me but she won't leave her name. I think it's Robin."

I just shrugged. "Can I, Mom?" I asked again. "Everyone is going."

"Who's everyone?" Mark said, like he had to be the dad all of a sudden.

"Will you hush up?" I said. "Why are you being such a brat? Can I, Mom?"

"If you want to," Mom said. "I presume that her parents are going to be there?"

I rolled my eyes. "Duh!" I said. But then I quick added, "Sorry! I mean yes, they are."

I saw Mom and Dad exchange looks and I could tell they were both trying not to laugh.

Parents are so weird. Sometimes, you say something fresh, or not even fresh, just a little smart, and you get grounded for an entire week. Other times — like now — they think you're funny.

"Where's Meg, Alex?" Mom asked. "I hope you were watching her this afternoon — taking *good* care of her? Your Friday job? And by the way, I don't know if Dad and I have told you enough how pleased we are at how you've been acting this past week."

"Really pleased," Daddy added. "Like now — you remembered to put your bike away before dark." He smiled at me. "I think you're well on your way to that A."

Right.

I looked down at my sneakers. "Meg's upstairs in her room," I said. "We were together all afternoon practically."

"Well, go up and call her for dinner, will you?" Mom said.

"It's all right," Dad said. "I'm going upstairs to change anyway. I'll get her. Be down in two minutes."

But it was a lot less than two minutes — maybe thirty seconds — when he was back down. With Meg in his arms. Meg whose face was practically purple and was blown up about twice its normal size.

"I think we'd better get her to the doctor," Dad said, pressing Meg close to him, one hand holding her head against his chest. "She looks awful."

"I'd awdight!" Meg said. "Dop id."

But she didn't look all right. She looked like a Halloween pumpkin. Or a basketball.

Even from across the room, I could hear her breathing. Every time she breathed, there was this whistle, like a mini freight train had come through the kitchen.

I was suddenly terrified.

"Meg!" Mom said. "What happened?"

Without waiting for an answer, Mom turned to the cabinet and reached to the top shelf where she keeps the special medicine that Meg takes when she's having a really bad attack — cortisone, it's called.

Mom turned with the dropper already in her hand, filled with medicine. Dad set Meg down on the counter, and Meg opened her mouth like a baby bird, and Mom dropped the medicine in.

Mom and Dad and Mark and I all waited, watching Meg like she was a balloon about to burst.

I could feel my heart pounding like crazy in my chest. And suddenly Mark came and stood beside me, and I felt him reach for my hand.

Was he just comforting me? Or was he as scared as I was?

I felt myself blinking back tears. What if something bad happened to Meg, something really bad? And what if it was all my fault!

Oh, why had I let her near those cats?

But as we watched, like magic, suddenly Meg's color began to get more regular looking. I could see the purple fading out and becoming plain red, and then pink, and then, after a little while, she was almost normal-looking again. Even the puffiness began to go down. Then, after another minute or two, her breathing began being better, too, not all wheezy sound-ing.

I found myself taking a big breath, as though I had been holding it in, not even aware I'd been doing it. Next to me, I could hear Mark take a big breath, too.

"What happened, Meg?" Mom said. "What caused this? Do you know? Did you eat some-thing you shouldn't?"

For a minute, Meg didn't answer, and I al-most hoped she'd tell the truth. I couldn't bear the thought of her getting in trouble because of me.

But then Mom shook her head. "I think it's time she went back to the allergist anyway," Mom said, turning to Dad. "There have been too many of these attacks lately, for no reason."

"There's a reason," Meg said.

"Oh?" Mom said.

"Pizza," Mark said suddenly. "She had pizza."

"Pizza?" Mom said. "Where'd she get pizza?"

"My fault," Mark said.

I turned and stared at him, and Mom and Dad did, too.

"I was making myself a frozen pizza before," he said, "and she came down and asked for a bite. I felt sorry for her. She's just a little kid and she can't eat anything, hardly. I didn't know it would hurt her. There was just a little bit of tomato on it. And I guess some cheese."

"Honestly, Mark!" Mom said, and she pressed her hands on either side of her head like she does sometimes — mostly because of something I did — like she's trying to keep her head from flying apart.

But I could tell she felt sorry for Mark, too, because after a minute, she came over and ruffled his hair. "It's all right," she said to him softly. "You didn't mean to. But do be more careful from now on. Look at her!"

"Well, at least we know," Dad said. "And I think we'd better give Meg her allergy diet tonight. Tuna fish and rice for you tonight, Miss Meg."

That's when I knew there would be more trouble. Because I had taken the last cans of

tuna fish to the cats, cats who were still hanging out in the garage.

And somehow I had to get them down,
bagged and returned — and I had less than an
hour left to do it in.

Four

At least one thing went right that day. There were some cans of tuna for Meg's dinner because Mom had bought some when she did the grocery shopping. She didn't even seem to notice any were missing. She just opened one of the cans and went about getting rice ready. The rice was going to take a while to cook, so I had time to go upstairs to pack a bag — and to call Elizabeth. I just stuffed my pajamas and toothbrush and clean underwear inside my sleeping bag, and then picked up the phone.

In case I couldn't get the cats before Elizabeth picked me up, I had to ask her to sneak back with me during the night to help.

"Oh, Alex!" Elizabeth said as soon as she heard it was me on the phone. "Guess what? Robin called again. There's going to be *boys* there tonight, her big brother Ryan's friends, not for a sleepover but a pizza party, because Ryan was disappointed about not going to the horse farm, too, and he said it wasn't fair that Robin got to have a sleepover and he didn't get anything, you know how spoiled he is, so their mom is letting him have a party, too, with all of his friends. And one of the boys is guess who? Oh, you'll never guess, but you know Ryan's friend, Matt Murphy? Matt is such . . . well, the most gorgeous and he's so mature. I think he's as old as your brother, Mark, maybe older, maybe even thirteen. And all I have to wear is my regular ratty old stuff that Matt sees all the time at school, so I asked my sister, Melinda — not Susan, she's such a brat — if I could borrow her black angora sweater and she said, 'Over my dead body.' I mean, Melinda's such a brat, too, like they both are. She said I smell up her clothes when I borrow them and I don't at all. Even though I begged, she said she'd kill me if I even came near her room, but I don't think she really meant it, so anyway, she went out with her friends to the movies before, and just now I snuck in and took the sweater and, this is really weird, but I kept looking around when I went in there, you know, like there was really a dead body there that I'd have to step over to get to the sweater? Well, of course, there wasn't. And then tonight, after Matt leaves, we can just sneak back here and put the sweater back in her dresser and she'll never know, and then we can go back to Robin's, and you'll help me, won't you?"

She paused and I could hear her take a deep breath.

I didn't answer for a minute, not because I didn't have an answer, but because I had to catch my breath. When Elizabeth gets in one of those talking frenzies, she makes me feel like I can't breathe, either.

"Alex?" she said. "You there? You hear me? And did you call Robin and tell her you're coming? She said you hadn't called her yet. But I told her you were coming. You are, aren't you? Yes, you are."

It's true. I hadn't called Robin. Between Meg, and her allergies, and the cats, I had totally forgotten about calling.

"I'm going," I said. "I'll call her right now. Did she say anything about the cats?"

"Cats? What cats? Oh, those cats! No, she didn't say anything. She probably hadn't even noticed they were missing. Did you get them back okay?"

"No," I said. "I didn't get them back okay. I didn't get them back at all. I need you to help me."

For the first time there was silence. A *long* silence.

"I know you're there," I said. "If I help with the sweater, will you help with the cats?"

"You didn't get the cats back?" she yelled. "Why not? She'll kill you if she finds out!"

"Thanks," I said.

"It's true!" she said. "So how come? I mean, how come you didn't put them back yet?"

"Because the stupid cats think they're birds. They're perched up on the rafters in my garage and won't come down."

"Oh, is that all?" Elizabeth said. "That's easy. Just get a ladder and climb up there and you can coax them with something, maybe those cat treats like Pounce or something. If you put Pounce up on the rafters, then you can get the cats to — "

"*Hush!*" I said.

She hushed. For a long time.

"What?" she said after a while, almost in a whisper.

"I tried that," I said. "Not Pounce, but tuna fish. And I couldn't get them to do anything, to come anywhere near me. I even stood on Dad's precious workbench and if he caught me there I'd be killed. But if we do it together, I can go to one end of the rafter, and you can be down at the other end. And that way, no matter which way they run, we can capture them."

Again, silence.

"Okay," Elizabeth said finally. "If you can help me, I can help you. Anyhow, it's probably safer returning the cats than returning Melinda's sweater."

"Maybe," I said. Then I heard Mom calling me for dinner, and I added, "I got to go. We're going to eat. Mom's calling."

"Want me to call Robin for you?" Elizabeth asked. "Tell her you're coming?"

"Yeah," I said. "Just tell her I said I'm coming but I didn't have time to call."

"Sure," she said. She paused and then added quietly, "It's going to be hard to act surprised if she tells me her cats are missing."

"I know," I said. "Me, too."

"What should I say if she tells me that?" Elizabeth asked. "And what are we going to do about our project?"

"How do I know?" I said. I sighed. "Tell her you heard Alex was in the neighborhood eyeing her cats."

"Really?" she said.

"Of course not really! You sound like Meg."

"Meg's nice," Elizabeth said, sounding like her feelings were hurt.

I felt bad. "I know Meg's nice," I said. "What time will you be here?"

"Half an hour? Seven-thirty, Robin said."

Half an hour! Half an hour to eat dinner. Half an hour to act like nothing was wrong. Half an hour to eat dinner, act like nothing was wrong, and sneak to the garage and capture the cats! And even when I succeeded with that . . .

Oh, well.

"Say a prayer," I said. "And start some creative thinking. We have a project due Monday."

We said good-bye then, and I went downstairs to dinner.

When we all sat down at the table, I took a good look at Meg. She looked back at me and grinned. I was so happy to see that she seemed just like normal, that her face was pink and regular and not at all swollen. I couldn't even hear her breathing. I felt so relieved.

Meg can be a real pain, but she is nice. And sometimes, like now, her face is so sweet and so sort of *new* looking, it surprises me into some feeling I can't really explain. It's a nice but totally weird feeling.

When everybody was served, we all bent our heads for a silent prayer and took each other's hands.

Mark is always on my right, and Daddy on my left.

Most nights, I hate that silent prayer. It used to be that Mark was such a jerk, squeezing my hand too tight, or else, like one night, he had a bloodworm hidden in the palm of the hand I had to take. And when I complained, Mom and Dad would tell me to hush and pray. But at least there was always something happening, especially when I found ways of getting even.

Lately though, since he's become Mr. Wonderful, he doesn't even try to do stupid things. Like the other night, when I had Jell-O smeared on my hand and I was going to tell him it was slug slime, he just shook his head and got up and went to the kitchen and washed his hands.

Tonight I was glad of the silent time and glad

that neither of us had tricks, because I had some praying to do. Mom and Dad always say God isn't like Santa Claus, someone you ask for presents and stuff. They say I can ask for help, but I should expect that God will choose what is good for me. And they say that if there's nothing special to say, I should simply direct my thoughts to God and be quiet, that God will inspire me with good thoughts and wisdom.

Most nights, I don't have any good thoughts, and I sure don't have any wisdom. But tonight, I did need prayers. There were two cats out there in the garage that I definitely needed help with. I had to show I was grown-up. I really *wanted* to be grown-up, responsible. Like Mark.

And then, in the silence of that prayer time, I heard a definite, and very loud, "Meow!"

I looked up and saw Meg looking at me.

She had heard, too.

But Mom and Dad and even Mark still had their heads bent, eyes closed, holding hands. Mark looked very fervent.

Had the cats escaped? Were they roaming around the yard? Surely I wouldn't have heard them all the way from the garage? Then they must have escaped!

I closed my eyes and prayed harder: Don't let the cats have escaped. Even if you're not like Santa, please answer this prayer!

In a minute, all of us opened our eyes and let go of each others' hands. No one but Meg and me seemed like we were listening for cat sounds.

After we were all served, Daddy started talking about some poor person he was defending. It was a man who was retarded and couldn't read or write, and was so confused he couldn't even understand exactly what it was he was accused of. Mom and Mark got all involved in the conversation.

All I could think was: Was Dad really a good lawyer? Would he be allowed to defend his own daughter? Or was that against the law?

"Oh, by the way," Dad said, turning to me. "Talking about confusion — there was a message for you on the answering machine before that I forgot to tell you about. A strange one."

"You mean Robin?" I said. "I know about it. I listened. Actually, Elizabeth told me, too."

"Really?" Dad looked puzzled. "Robin seemed to be saying it was a big secret."

"The sleepover?" I said.

Dad shook his head. "No, something else, I

think. I'm not sure. I wrote it down for you —
something about a secret? Go out in the
kitchen and look."

"She can look later," Mom said. "We're eating."

But I was already up and had left the table
and gone to the kitchen.

There, by the telephone, was the notepad.
And a note in Dad's handwriting.

*Alex: Robin called. Secrets. No one
knows but you and me. Also, glad your
dad's a lawyer! Bring stuff tonight.*

The note was signed, *Dad*. With this P.S.:
And what's <u>this</u> all about?

As if I knew! Bring *what* stuff? The cats?
Did she know? Is that why she said, "glad your
dad's a lawyer"?

I tried to replay the message, but someone
had rewound the tape and all I got was a repeat
of someone for Mark.

I went back into the dining room, feeling so
weak I just plopped down in my chair.

"Something wrong, sweetie?" Mom asked,
looking up and frowning at me.

"No. Weird message, though."

"I'll say," Dad said, laughing. " 'Glad your dad's a lawyer,' she said. You girls aren't in trouble or anything, are you?"

But I could tell from the way he said that, that he didn't mean it at all, that he thought it was a big joke.

I looked over at Meg and she looked back at me.

Some joke! I thought.

Meg was mouthing something, a worried look on her face.

I knew exactly what she was mouthing, asking me: Am I an accessory?

She was.

But that was nothing. Nothing compared to the trouble I was in if those cats had escaped and I couldn't get them back.

Five

I gobbled my dinner as fast as I could, but I didn't do it so fast that Mom would notice. If she sees me eating fast, she makes me slow down and sit quietly for a while. As soon as I was finished, I asked to be excused to pack for the overnight, even though I had done that already. I had to make one more attempt at capturing the cats — whether they were in or out of the garage. If I could catch them, I could just run around the block with them, dump them over Robin's fence, and be back home by the time Elizabeth and her mom stopped by for me. Then, as soon as we got to Robin's, Elizabeth and I could ask to see the cats and when they weren't in the garage, we could all search the yard and find them. I was sure they wouldn't have climbed out of Robin's yard and over her fence in that short a while. Besides, that privacy fence they put up for the new swimming pool is huge.

If only the cats would cooperate! If only they were there! All I had was about five minutes.

Our house is very big, with a long stairway in the front hall that leads to the upstairs hall and front bedrooms where Mom and Dad and Meg and I have our rooms. And then there's a back staircase that comes down from the back hall where Mark has two whole rooms to himself. Mom says that a long time ago, when the first owners built this house, those back rooms used to be maids' rooms. Our family doesn't have maids. Anyway, because the rooms are so small back there, Mark gets to have two rooms, one to sleep in, and one for a study or playroom. I think it's totally unfair that he has two rooms, but Dad says it's fair because Mark is the oldest. So? It's not my fault that I wasn't born first.

When I told Dad that, he said if I could figure out a way to be the firstborn, I could get two rooms, too.

Very funny!

That night when I was excused from dinner, I made a lot of noise going up the front stairs. Then, once I was up there, very quietly I went across the hall and circled around to the back stairs. I tiptoed down them, holding my breath. I could still hear the family in the dining room. Quietly, I opened the back door and slipped out into the dark yard.

It was cold out, and I had no coat. I raced across the yard, and to the garage, hugging myself to keep warm.

I hoped the cats were warm enough, but I figured they probably were all right in their fur coats.

I looked up at the stars. It was such a beautiful night. If the cats were safe, I could enjoy it.

When I got to the garage, though, I saw something that made me almost cry right there on the spot — the side door was opened, blowing slowly back and forth in the wind.

I had closed it. I *knew* I had closed it. And now the cats were probably gone!

I ran in, pulling the door shut behind me and leaning against it.

"Are you here, kitties?" I murmured. "Here, kitty, kitty. Oh, please, be here."

I held my breath, listening for the rustle of cats.

Nothing. No sound at all.

I didn't dare turn on the light, in case Mom or Dad saw it from the dining room window.

"Here, kitty, kitty," I whispered again. "Kitty? *Kitties?* Oh, please, be here!"

Absolute silence. They had escaped. And Robin *knew* it was me who stole them. Felony. Larceny. Big trouble. Jail. A record.

No A.

And then, suddenly, something brushed against my leg — two somethings, so soft, so silent, so wrap-around-my-legs, that for a moment, they scared me half to death.

Cats! Cats, one on either side of me, circling my legs, round and round.

They hadn't escaped! But they must have! How else could I have heard them in the dining room? But then they must have come back.

I thought of saying a thank-you prayer, but I figured that God had nothing to do with this. I was pretty sure he didn't help thieves.

I reached down for the cats, and it was then that I realized that I had to turn on the light. There was no way I could capture these cats in the dark.

Or could I? Maybe if I moved slowly . . .

I crouched down, super-superslowly.

The two cats were still circling my legs.

"Nice kitty," I whispered. "Two nice kitties."

I could feel them, twining round and round my legs.

"Nice kitty," I whispered.

I reached down, pretending to try and pat them — but the minute my hand touched one, they were gone.

Not a single breath, not a sound, nothing circling round, nothing brushing against me.

Stupid, mind-reading cats!

"Where are you?" I whispered.

No sound. No movement at all.

I had to try the light.

Praying, praying that no one in the house was looking, I found the light switch, and flicked it on. At the same moment, both cats leapt for the workbench.

Fortunately, though, they didn't knock over any of Dad's tools or that rocking horse. And they didn't continue up onto the rafters.

They just stalked along the workbench, looking at me over their shoulders — or whatever that part of them is.

Slowly, I followed them, my hand stretched out. "Here, kitties," I said.

They both stood watching me, that we-don't-trust-you-for-a-minute look on their little cat faces.

"It's all right," I assured them.

Ha! The cat snatcher comes closer.

I took another step.

But just as I got close enough to try and make a grab for them, both of them leapt for the rafters.

"All right! Go ahead!" I called to them. "See if I care! You'll starve to death in here."

And I turned off the light, went out, and pulled the garage door tight. I tested to be sure it was closed tight. Then I ran back across the lawn to the house.

Already, I could see lights turning up the driveway — Elizabeth's mom's car, I bet.

I ran in the back way, ran on tiptoe up the back stairs, grabbed my clothes and sleeping bag, then pounded down the front stairs to open the door.

" 'Bye, Mom! 'Bye, Dad!" I yelled. "Elizabeth's mom is here!"

I heard them all call "Good-bye," and I think

Mom was saying something about kissing her good-bye, but I ran out and jumped in the car.

I said hi to Elizabeth and to her mom and in two seconds we were around the corner at Robin's, saying good-bye and heading up to the house. It's really dumb, but Elizabeth's mom won't let her walk anywhere after dark, insists on driving her — even if it is just around the corner.

"Any luck?" Elizabeth asked as we went up the walk.

Two words. The shortest sentence Elizabeth has ever said in her whole entire life.

"None," I said. "But at least they're still in the garage. For a minute before, I thought they had run away."

"Oh, man!" Elizabeth whispered. "You'd be in so much trouble if they had, I mean those are really expensive cats and you know how — "

"Shush!" I said.

At that moment Robin opened the door, and her mom, Mrs. Thatcher, and most of the girls in the fifth grade were there in the hall behind her, calling and yelling and laughing. Well,

Mrs. Thatcher wasn't yelling and laughing, but everybody else was.

Mrs. Thatcher is kind of scary-looking — perfectly dressed always, every hair in place, lipstick perfect, nails perfect, shiny, red, long, and bent like dragon claws. And she always, always, always wears high heels. Once, when I slept over Robin's, I got up to go to the bathroom in the middle of the night and I passed Mrs. Thatcher in the hall. She was wearing a robe and nightgown, and slippers with high, high heels. Even dressed for bed like that, she looked like she was ready to go to a PTA meeting or something.

Now, as soon we walked in, Robin grabbed my hand and began pulling me behind her into the living room.

Her mother, coming with us!

"The rest of you go in the family room!" Robin called. "We'll be right there! Stay out of the basement. The boys are there."

I saw Elizabeth watching me being pulled along, and from the look on her face, it seemed like she was about to faint.

But there was nothing to do but follow Robin. The others went to the family room —

or I bet to the basement where the boys were —
and then Robin and the dragon lady and I were
alone in the living room.

"Alex!" Mrs. Thatcher said very solemnly,
"did you get our message?"

"*My* message?" Robin said, frowning at her
mom.

My tongue was stuck to the roof of my
mouth, so that when I tried to speak, all that
came out was a little squeak.

Robin didn't seem to notice. "About the secret?" she said.

"A surprise, actually," Mrs. Thatcher said.
"Quite a surprise."

What did they mean? If they knew, why
didn't they just come out and say so?

I looked at Mrs. Thatcher and for some reason, thought of my mom then — Mom who is
always at the agency working with sick babies,
and even sometimes bringing them home and
trying to find homes for them. Mom is pretty,
but kind of casual-looking — well, *very* casual-
looking, compared to Mrs. Thatcher. Mom's
hair is often drooping in her eyes, and I always
think she looks like she's about to lose parts
of herself — her eyeglasses on a chain around

her neck hanging loose, her loafers drooping off the backs of her heels, her briefcase strap sliding down her arm.

Why did I think of Mom now? Because I wished she was here! I felt like a complete baby. Oh, why had I ever thought I could get away with stealing Robin's cats?

"Is something wrong, my dear?" Mrs. Thatcher asked.

She calls everybody, "My dear," and even though it should sound nice, it always sounds scary to me.

"No. Nothing," I whispered.

"Your voice?" Mrs. Thatcher said.

I cleared my throat, but it didn't help much. "It's just changing," I said.

I knew girls' voices didn't change, but I remembered what was happening to Mark's voice and it was all I could think of for the moment.

"My dear," Mrs. Thatcher said, leaning forward very confidentially, "girls' voices don't change!"

"Well, maybe mine will," I whispered back. "I mean, maybe because I have a boy's name. I mean, because . . ."

I was babbling. I was stupid.

I was in trouble.

"Listen, and stop being silly," Robin said. "This is the secret. Mom and Dad are taking us to Disney World this spring, and we can each take a friend — "

"Only if you and Ryan get good report cards for the winter term, my dear!" Mrs. Thatcher interrupted.

"I know, Mom!" Robin said, rolling her eyes at her mom. "Anyway," Robin said to me, "we're each allowed to bring one friend. And I'm bringing you!"

"How come?" I said. "I mean — "

I stopped. I knew what I had just said wasn't very polite, but it had just popped out.

Robin was the Popularity Princess. Everybody wanted to be her best friend. Yet I didn't even like her very much and I was pretty sure she didn't like me all that much, either.

Robin didn't seem mad at my question, though. She just smiled and shrugged.

"And your brother, Mark, will be Ryan's guest," Mrs. Thatcher added.

Oh.

Really?

Ryan doesn't have many friends, and he's always trying to get Mark to do things with him, calling Mark all the time. But I know Mark doesn't like Ryan. They play soccer together, and Mark says Ryan isn't a "team player" — about the meanest thing I've ever heard Mark say about anybody. So I didn't think for a minute Mark would be Ryan's guest.

"Well, it's not definite yet," Mrs. Thatcher said, like she knew what I was thinking. "I know Mark has to work out some things at home. But he will."

Then, suddenly, I thought I knew why *I* was being asked. And it was all about Mark. See, after school each day, Mark and I are on our own till Mom and Dad get home from work. Still, Mom always says that if there's a problem, Mark is the one who is "in charge." If I went, then Mark wouldn't have to be "in charge" so he'd be free to go, too. I bet anything, Mark had already refused and used the excuse that it was because of me. If I came, then Ryan could get Mark to go.

But much more important: *Robin* could get Mark.

As if to confirm my thought, Mrs. Thatcher said, "So if you came, then Mark would be free to come also."

"But that's not the only reason!" Robin said quickly, linking her arm through my arm and making a face at her mom. "I mean, we're not asking you because you and Mark have to go together like a package or something. It's that you're one of my best friends."

"Yes. You and your brother are such charming children," Mrs. Thatcher said. "You'll make such a nice addition to our table. We stay at a very exclusive club when we're there."

Addition to her *table*? It sounded like she was planning to eat us!

"Mom, really!" Robin said, and she stretched out the word *really* like she was totally annoyed. She turned to me then. "We'll do everything together from now on, all right? We'll be best friends."

I did not want to be Robin's best friend. Not at all. And I did not want to go on any vacation with her, even though I've always wanted to go to Disney World.

But I was feeling very relieved that this had nothing to do with stolen cats.

And, suddenly, I remembered the rest of that message . . . "Glad your dad's a lawyer."

I had to know what that was about, even if it was about the cats. I couldn't stand not knowing. I was also going to say that I didn't want to go to Disney World, but I was going to say it in a nice way.

"The . . . lawyer part?" I said.

Robin blushed and turned to the door.

"Let's go," she said.

I followed her out of the living room and toward the family room.

"My mom's weird sometimes," Robin said when we were out of earshot of her mom.

"About lawyers?" I said.

Robin just shrugged.

"What about them?" I persisted.

"Nothing."

"But you said — "

"Forget it!" she said. "I mean it! Just let's forget it, all right? Really!" She said it just the way she did to her mom, and then rolled her eyes, just like at her mom.

I wondered if anyone's eyes ever got stuck up in their heads when they did that.

"Well, you're the one who brought it up!" I said.

"Well, it's not important, okay?" she said. "It's just that Mom — well, she just wants our friends, especially our guests, to be the children of professionals." Robin put on a fake, snooty voice when she said the word *professionals.* "So your dad's a professional, okay?"

My mom's a professional, too, I thought, but I didn't say that.

"How come?" I said.

Robin shrugged. "How do I know?" she said. And she sounded mad. For the first time ever, I wondered if she felt sad sometimes, stuck with a mother like that.

"Come on, let's go," Robin said, and she took my arm and pulled me into the family room. "We're going to Disney World, that's what counts."

"I . . . don't think so," I said. "I mean, thanks anyway, but I think — "

"Maybe in Florida," Robin interrupted, looking right at my naked ears, "you can finally have your ears pierced like the rest of us. My mom will go with you if you want."

She would?

I bet Mom would give me money to spend at

Disney World. I could use some of it for my ears. I wouldn't have to save up from baby-sitting. But did I want to go to Disney World with Robin for a whole week just to have my ears pierced? No. There were better ways to get money and have my ears pierced than to spend a week with the Popularity Princess.

Before I could say anything, though, we were in the family room, and Robin yelled, "Hey, everybody! Everybody ready for the pet project? I was going to do my horse, but I decided on cats. Have you all seen my cats, Mootsie and Tootsie? They're really beautiful."

"Oooh, yeah!" somebody cooed.

"They really are cute!" Marcy said. "Where are they now?"

"They're mostly outdoor cats," Robin said. "We keep them out except at night. They're in the garage."

Want to bet? I thought.

Elizabeth and I exchanged looks.

"I'll show them to you!" Robin said. She turned to me and linked her arm through mine again. "Come on with me," she said. "We're going to do everything together from now on, like I said. Let's get the cats."

"Well . . . no . . . I don't think so," I said. "I mean I would but . . ."

But there wasn't much sense stalling. She was going to find out sooner or later. And it seemed to be sooner, as she pulled hard on my arm, dragging me toward the back door. The yard. And the empty garage.

Six

"Wait!" Elizabeth said suddenly. "Alex and I will do it. We have a surprise, something we left outside anyway, we'll get it, all right, you all just wait here, it's a big surprise that we've been waiting for weeks to show you and we made it ourselves even though there wasn't any . . . any pattern, I mean, menu, no, recipe, see because if anybody could do this, we could because we know all about how peanut butter and jelly and . . . and snowflakes and apples work with this. . . ."

She would have gone on making no sense. But nobody noticed because suddenly nobody was listening to her at all — not listening because some of Ryan's friends had come up from the basement and into the family room.

There were just three of them, but they were the three that all the girls think are gorgeous — Robert Wright, Tim Moynihan, and Matt Murphy. Matt has this sort of sideways grin that everybody flips about. Not me, though. I think he looks kind of sinister.

I saw Elizabeth swallow and then her hand went to smooth her sweater, her sister Melinda's stolen black angora sweater.

Be still my heart! I thought.

But then I suddenly realized — forget the guys. This was the perfect opportunity. While everybody was flirting with them, we could sneak out and capture the cats.

"Elizabeth!" I whispered.

She didn't budge, didn't even seem to hear me. She was just staring at Matt.

"Elizabeth!" I said again.

Still she stood there, one hand pressed to her chest and Melinda's sweater.

"Elizabeth!" I said firmly.

She turned and looked at me.

I motioned with my head to the door.

She sighed softly, gave one more look at Matt, then turned and followed me out.

A real friend.

She had stolen her sister's angora sweater, and didn't even get a chance to show it off to Matt.

In my mind, I promised her I'd make it up to her.

Both of us fled to the hall, grabbed our coats, and were out the front door.

As soon as we were outside, Elizabeth started. "What happened with her mom before, does her mom know, what did she say to you in there, did you *see* Matt?" All in one breath.

"She wants me to go to Disney World with her!" I said. "Actually, she wants Mark to go with Ryan because I think she's in love with Mark and so she asked me, and yes, I saw Matt and I'm sorry."

I shook my head. Sometimes I find myself talking like Elizabeth when I've been with her awhile.

"Disney World, why? I mean, you don't even like her!" Elizabeth said.

"Because of Mark. Anyway, it's a long story. I'll tell you more later," I said. "First, the cats."

We began running. It was cold out, and we hugged our coats to us as we ran — down the shortcut in the alley between Robin's house and the church, around the corner to my block, then across the street and around the side of my house. When we got in my yard, we stayed far enough away so that if anyone were looking out the windows they wouldn't see us.

The lawn was mushy from the damp and cold, and my feet were getting very wet.

But in just a minute, we were at the garage.

Fortunately, the door was still closed tightly.

We snuck in, then turned on the lights.

And there, right in front of us, right inside the door, curled up on their two pillowcases like they knew just where they were supposed to be, were both cats.

"So what was the big deal?" Elizabeth said, looking first at the cats, then at me. "They're not up on the rafters, look at them, they're right here in front of us, you silly."

"Hush!" I said.

I reached down slowly, very slowly, expecting them to leap up and fly away like before.

But they were as docile as could be, both of them lying there purring as we reached to pat them.

"You take one, and I'll take one," I said softly.

"Just slide him into the pillowcase and then hold him close so he won't escape. I told you I read that cats get sleepy inside pillowcases, and it's true. It happened before this afternoon. They fell right asleep and didn't even scratch."

That wasn't exactly true. One of them fell asleep and didn't scratch. And one of them stayed awake and tried its best to get me. But I didn't tell her that, and I didn't tell her that I didn't know which one was which, either.

"They better *not* scratch," Elizabeth said. "Melinda will kill me if I get a hole in her sweater, I mean it, she will, too."

She reached for the cat closest to her and scooped it up, cradling it in two hands like a bag of potatoes or something.

I scooped up my cat, too.

Both of us were able to slip our cats into their bags very easily.

"So why didn't you let me do this before?" I muttered to them as we stood up, the cats snuggled against our coats.

"Ready?" Elizabeth asked, her hand on the light switch. "I'm ready, are you?"

I nodded, but suddenly, I noticed something.

And from the look on Elizabeth's face, I could tell she did, too. "It stinks in here," she said.

"Tuna fish," I said.

"Throw-up, cat throw-up," she answered.

"Never mind," I said. "I'll clean it up later."

"What if your dad comes out to his workshop?"

"He comes out on Sunday, mostly," I said. "That's his workday."

But while I was talking I was walking around — carefully — trying to see if I could find where they had made their mess. And feeling my cat moving against my side, anything but asleep.

It started meowing suddenly, a funny sound, like it was asking a question.

I looked at Elizabeth, and she looked at me, and we both started to laugh.

It was such a pitiful, questioning sound. "Meow?" it said. "Meee-owww??"

But then I stopped laughing. Because I saw where the cats had made their mess. And it was *not* funny.

There was cat throw-up all over the floor beside Dad's workbench. But that wasn't the worst of it. There was cat throw-up *on the rock-*

ing horse Dad had just finished for Mom's office. The horse was lying on its side, its fringed leather mane spread out, as Dad had left it for the glue to dry. And there was definitely cat throw-up, lumps of tuna fish it looked like, stuck on the horse's mane.

"Stupid cats!" I said, and my cat jumped and its claws came sticking through the bag.

I held it out at arm's length.

"Look at that!" I said to Elizabeth, pointing.

"Ohmigosh, ohmigosh, ohmi*gosh*areyouintrouble!" she said. "What are you going to do?"

Do. Do. I was thinking fast, but nothing came to me. Dad would have a fit! I'd be grounded for a year, till I was as old as Grandma, till I died, till eternity maybe.

And I could forget baby-sitting and that A!

"We could just say that some neighbor cats got in here," Elizabeth said, looking very innocent and wide-eyed. "It's the truth, you know, they did, so it wouldn't be a lie at all, not really!"

I shook my head. "I'd be in just as much trouble. I'm supposed to close up the garage. It's my job when I put away my bike at night."

Elizabeth came closer to the workbench, her

cat held close to her side. Her cat was absolutely still.

Lucky her. She had gotten the sleepy one that Meg had this afternoon.

We both stood looking down at the mess. "We can clean up the floor," Elizabeth said, "but there's no way we could cut out that mess, I mean, wash out that mess. The horse is ruined." She shuddered.

I looked at Elizabeth. "You said 'cut out' the mess," I said.

"I meant wash it out."

"Yes, but if we did cut it out, he'd never know . . ." I pointed to the horse. The mess was mostly right along the edge of the mane. "If we just cut the mane, made it about an inch shorter, Dad would probably not even notice."

"Probably," Elizabeth said.

"Think so?" I said.

"Maybe," Elizabeth said. "But wouldn't washing it be better? I mean, like we should try it?"

I'd need soap. I looked around. There was probably some around here somewhere. But there was no water.

"I could go in the house for water and soap,"

I said. "I could sneak in the kitchen way. I can tell by the lights if anyone's in the kitchen."

"Do we have time?" Elizabeth asked.

"No," I said.

We both looked at each other.

"Cut it?" I asked.

Elizabeth nodded. "You don't have to cut much," she said.

"Right," I said.

"Go for it!" Elizabeth said. "I'll hold your cat."

I handed it to her, and she held it very gingerly, at arm's length. It was squirming and meowing like crazy.

I went to Dad's workbench, stepping carefully over the mess on the floor.

It really wouldn't be too hard to clean up the floor later or even tomorrow. Cement isn't like a leather mane. It would be easy to scrub up.

Dad has all his tools arranged in order, each one in a slot that fits it precisely.

I found the scissors in no time at all, big ones. And at the same time, I found a pair of gardening gloves.

Great! I put them on so I wouldn't have to worry about cat stuff on my hands. Then I carefully took down the scissors and bent over the horse's mane.

"Be careful," Meg said quietly.

"I will," I said, and I began cutting.

I cut the whole length of the mane, starting at the horse's head and working backward, cutting very carefully. I took just about one inch off the whole thing, then stood back and looked at it. Well, maybe two inches. More even. In places.

I looked at Elizabeth. "What do you think?"

"It's all right," she said. But I could see she was biting her lip. And then she clamped her lips shut and made this hiccuping sound.

I gathered up the cut parts of the mane and threw them in a trash bin that Dad keeps next to the bench.

"What?" I asked.

"Very . . ." She swallowed hard. "Very . . ."

I glared at her. "What?" I asked again.

"Very punk looking?" she said. And it all came out in a funny, high-pitched voice, like she was trying so hard not to laugh.

She took a deep breath. "But I like it!" she added quickly. "Really. I always liked . . . punk-looking rocking horses." She swallowed again. "When I was a kid."

She handed me the squirming cat. "Let's go. We're going to be in trouble."

Going to be in trouble?

And what'd she think *this* was?

We were out of there.

Running across the back lawn. Across the street. Around the corner. Down the alley behind Robin's house.

And all the time, my cat was meowing like mad.

"Shush up!" I whispered. "You'll be home in a minute."

When we got to the big fence around Robin's yard, we stopped. It was pitch-dark in the alley, near the very back part of her yard.

We could just see the outline of the garage, all enclosed by the fence, and the big hole where they were digging the swimming pool.

"We'll just drop them over the fence," I said softly. "No way am I climbing over to get into the garage, like I did this afternoon."

"Yeah," Elizabeth said. "She'll just think the garage door swung open all by itself, like the wind did it or something, you know how the wind does that sometimes, and she'll think they got into the yard that way, did you leave the garage door open, like the side door or anything?"

Did I?

"No," I said. "But don't worry, she won't fig-ure it out. Come on, let's do it."

We hoisted up our cats.

The fence was as high as our heads, but it wasn't hard to lift the cats up that high. In the dark, I fumbled around, trying to slide the cat down to the open end of the pillowcase — do it and not get scratched to death. It took a minute, but eventually I had it the right way and I shook it, trying to shake the cat out and into the yard. "There you go!" I said.

"You, too!" Elizabeth said to her cat.

My arms were stretched over my head, and the cat and the pillowcase were hanging over inside the fence. It was so high I couldn't see over. I could tell this, though: Even though I was shaking and shaking, that cat was not moving.

Its claws must have been stuck to the pil-lowcase.

"Get!" I said to him.

He didn't. I could still feel his weight, feel him clinging to the pillowcase, and he was meowing like crazy.

"Go!" I said. "Get!"

"What's your problem?" Elizabeth whispered. "Hurry up! They're going to miss us!"

"He won't go!" I said.

"What do you mean, he won't go? Let go!" She shook my arm, like it was me who was holding on to the cat, not like the cat was holding on to me. And as she shook my arm, the cat dropped free — free and over the fence. Over the fence and into the yard.

The cat was free!

I was free!

"How did you get yours out of the pillowcase so easily?" I said.

"What do you mean, 'out'?" Elizabeth asked.

"Out!" I said. "Where's the pillowcase?"

"I dropped it in the yard, cat and all, what do you think?"

I just stared at her. "I don't believe you did that," I said.

"Why? What's the matter with that?" she said. "They won't figure it out, they'll think it's their pillowcase. Or the gardener will find it and he'll think it's a rag or something, you worry too much."

Too much? It was Mom's pillowcase. Mom's *monogrammed* pillowcase.

I didn't even answer.

But the truth was, I didn't care all that much right that minute. I was free. Free of those awful cats.

I stuck my pillowcase inside my jacket and we just raced back to Robin's house.

Back to Robin's house and in the front door.

And practically right into her mother's arms.

Seven

Mrs. Thatcher was standing at the door and was she mad! She said we were her responsibility for the night, and she had no intention of our running around the neighborhood, and she had half a mind to tell our parents, and, besides, she was going to watch and be sure no one got out the rest of the night, blah, blah, blah. She even hinted she might un-invite me to Disney World — which would have been just fine with me. Except for the pierced ears. But she watched me like a hawk for the rest of the night, so Elizabeth and I didn't get a chance to get out to the yard and get the pillowcase back. It also meant that Elizabeth didn't get a chance to sneak home to return the angora sweater.

I felt so bad about that! Elizabeth had risked a lot to go with me, and I hadn't been able to help her out at all.

The rest of that night stunk. Literally. Because even though the cats didn't get out of the yard, when Robin found them and brought them in the house, they kept on throwing up all over the place. One of them threw up in Marcy's backpack that was lying there on the family room floor. Everybody was grossed out, but especially Robin and her mom. Well, Marcy was pretty upset, too.

And even though nobody knew — yet — that it was all my fault, still, I felt terrible. I didn't know her cats were like Meg, allergic to everything, that they were on a special diet. And here I had given them all that canned fish. I did hope they wouldn't die — all because I had decided to take care of them!

Oh, well.

But now I had a new worry — what would happen when Dad went out to his workbench and if he'd notice the rocking horse had had a haircut.

There was one final stupid thing to deal with: In spite of all the trouble I'd gone to —

and gotten into — I still didn't have any cats or any pets at all to care for over the weekend. By next morning, I'd be carrying around an egg and acting like a stupid mother hen!

Early that next morning, Elizabeth and I got up before the rest of them were even awake. Elizabeth was still hoping to be able to smuggle her sister's sweater into her room before she woke up. We packed up our stuff and tiptoed out to the kitchen, and found that Mrs. Thatcher was up, sitting at the table, sipping coffee, wearing her high heels and robe. She said she was sorry we had to leave so early, but she didn't look sorry. You could tell she's not the kind of mom who really likes sleepover parties.

At the corner, Elizabeth and I said good-bye, and she ran one way and I ran the other. We promised to call with news later.

When I got home, I had to use my key to get in. The porch light was still on and the night-light was on downstairs. Everyone was still asleep — everyone but Meg, that is. The only sound was coming from her room — my TV. I thought of going out to the garage right away to clean up the cat mess, but I wanted to put away my stuff first and just have a minute to myself. Besides, Dad wouldn't be up for a long while yet, I knew. Saturday was his sleep-in day.

I went up the stairs and looked in Meg's room.

She had her back to me and was kneeling in front of the TV. She had my Barbie dolls — Ken and the clothes and everything — spread out all over the floor, her sticker collection carefully laid out beside them on the rug. Meg has been collecting stickers for ages, and I try to buy some for her when I have money. She particularly likes unicorn ones. I'm always careful to buy the kind that peel off easily, though, ever since what happened to Dad. Once, Meg plastered stickers all over Dad's briefcase — to make it pretty, she said. But for some reason, those stickers were practically impossible to get off, and when you did get them off, they left a big, sticky square mark underneath. For a long time, until Dad bought a new one, he walked around with part rainbow stickers, part peeled-off gummy stuff, plastered all over his briefcase.

I watched Meg quietly for a minute, so intent on whatever it was she was doing.

She must have been feeling better, because she wasn't wheezing or anything. She was wearing her pajamas with the feet, the soft, pink pajamas, and her hair was all mussed and fluffy and clinging in curls around her neck. Sometimes, when I see her in pajamas, all warm from sleep like that, I think about how I love her. I also think how nice it would be to be a little kid again. No worries.

"Hi, Meg!" I said.

She turned. "Hi, Alex!" she said. "Can we go out and see the cats? I won't touch them, I promise."

"Can't," I said. "I took them back last night."

"Back? Why? I like them!"

"Yeah, and they made you sick! It's a long story, but I couldn't keep them for the weekend. Now I'll have to carry an egg around the rest of the weekend."

"An egg?" she said.

"I told you yesterday. I have to carry it around all weekend pretending I'm a mother hen. Boy, I wish I didn't have to do this. Wish I had a pet of some sort."

Meg seemed to be thinking. "Me, too," she said. "I wish for a cat. Or a Barbie. I love yours."

"Yeah, well you can't have mine," I said.

I came in and plopped down on her bed. I lay back on the pillow, moving aside some of the stuffed animals. Meg's bed is crammed with so many animals, I don't know how she has room for herself. Each night, it takes her about an hour to get to bed because she has this ritual — each animal gets a turn sleeping next to her, and she has to move them around and make sure each is getting its turn in the proper order. Then, she has to be sure they have their heads sticking out from the covers so they can breathe, and that they have enough room.

I picked one up, a floppy, long-legged dog, and turned him over.

"That's Raggles," Meg said.

"I know!" I said.

Meg has had Raggles since she was a baby. He has long, floppy legs and droopy ears. When Meg was little, she carried him around by one leg all the time. Now, I could see that his leg was coming off, the stitching coming loose.

"He needs fixing, Meg," I said.

"I know," Meg said, sad-sounding.

"Want me to sew him up for you?" I asked. "I could do it."

Meg eyed me for a minute. Then she sighed. "No."

"Why? It won't hurt him," I said. "Stuffed animals don't feel pain."

"They do too!" she said. "They hate it when they fall out of bed."

"That's different," I said. "They don't feel it when they're getting sewn together. They're used to it because that's how they were made."

"You sure?" she asked.

"I'm sure."

She seemed to be thinking that over. But then she just shook her head and said, "No. It'll hurt him. Alex, are you getting an A about me?"

I sat up and patted the bed beside me. "Come over here and talk to me."

I moved over and Meg came running across the room.

She leapt onto the bed, bouncing down beside me. Then she threw herself backward onto the pillow and lay there looking up at the ceiling.

"Don't you worry," I said. "I'll get an A with you."

"I hope so," she said. "I don't like it when Daddy's mad and you're in trouble."

"I'm not in trouble anymore," I said, but I wasn't exactly sure of that, with what was waiting out there in the garage. "You just wait and see," I said. "Somehow I'll get an A in this science project. And I'll surely get an A with you. We're set!"

She snuggled close to me.

I looked at my watch — almost nine o'clock. At the instant of nine, I had to start with the egg.

I sat up and Meg did, too.

"Want to play with my Barbies?" Meg said.

"*Your* Barbies? They're *my* Barbies!"

"But I get to keep them till day after tomorrow," she said, sounding very smug.

"So?" I said. "They're still mine. I get them back Monday."

Meg scrambled off the bed and went over to the toys that were spread all around the TV. I watched her put Ken into the sports car, smoothing his hair down as she did.

She really did love those dolls.

She turned to me.

"Come on. Play!" she said.

I shook my head. "Got to go," I said. "Important work to do." I looked at my watch again and sighed. "Time to be a hen."

Eight

I went downstairs to get an egg from the refrigerator.

But then I remembered. I grabbed the dustpan and brush and a wet sponge and some spray Lysol.

I raced to the garage with them. It really took just a minute to clean up. The smell was almost gone, and most of the cat stuff had dried up enough to just sweep it up. I wiped the floor and bench, dumped everything in the trash, sponge and all, then sprayed the place with Lysol.

There. Everything was fine.

I took a look at the rocking horse. It was . . . okay. The mane was a little uneven, but not much. Maybe if I ruffled it a bit it would just look fluffy? I did. It really wasn't that bad. Dad would probably not even notice.

I went back to the house to begin the hen project. First I got out an egg. I held it in my left hand because I'm right-handed and then I got the notebook. We had to record our *feelings* about the egg every hour, starting with getting the egg from the refrigerator. We had to do it eight times during the day today, Saturday, and then eight more times tomorrow, Sunday.

Stupid project!

But I had the egg and I had the notebook and I might as well get it over with. So this was my first entry:

"Got an egg . . ."

I paused for a minute, wondering: What could anyone *feel* about an egg?

I wrote: "It feels cold."

I went into the den and lay down on the couch to watch TV, the egg lying on my stomach. The cold feeling even went through my shirt.

But after a while of being there, the egg began to warm up.

Why wait till ten o'clock? Maybe I could get

all the entries down in a hurry. And if I did, would it be fair to put the egg away for rest of the day? I mean, if I had enough entries, maybe I wouldn't have to care for it all day?

I'd have to think about that. Anyway, I had an idea for entry number two, so I wrote it down: "The egg feels warmer."

I settled back on the couch, just as the phone rang.

I jumped up, and the egg rolled off my stomach, bounced on the sofa pillow, and tumbled toward the floor. I reached out and snatched it back just in time, inches before it smashed on the floor.

Safe! I then switched the egg from my right hand to my left, and then remembered that I always pick up the phone with my left hand, and then I had to switch it back.

The phone had rung six times before I finally was able to pick it up.

It was Elizabeth.

"Do you have your stupid egg?" she said. "Isn't this the weirdest thing, and guess what, Melinda didn't even know I had her sweater, she stayed over at Mary Ellen's last night so I put it back and she'll never know. Unless it smells, but you don't think that's true, do you,

I mean, I smell just like everybody else, and I wear deodorant and all so how can I *smell* any *different?* Do you have your egg? Doesn't it feel weird, are you worried about it?"

"Worried about it?" I said, when she finally gave me a chance to speak. "Of course I'm not worried about it. I'm worried about getting an A, is all."

"If you get an A you get to go to Disney World?" she asked, laughing.

"I'm not going to Disney World," I said. And then I added, "Probably." Because I was thinking about the ear piercing.

"Probably?" she said.

"*Definitely,*" I said. "But I do need that A."

"So want to do something today?" Elizabeth asked. "We could go to the mall if we could get anyone to take us."

"And take our eggs with us?" I said.

"Oh. I forgot. But we could put them in our pockets, I bet they'd be all right there if we were wearing loose pants or something or maybe a skirt, maybe I could even borrow something from Melinda again, her jeans are bigger than mine and the pockets would be fine. I could even get a pair for you, you want me to? No, you're really tiny — "

"Elizabeth!" I said, very firmly, the only way to shut her up.

There was a pause, and then she whispered, "What?"

"We can't take an egg to the mall — not in our pockets, we can't!"

"Why not?"

"Because what if anyone saw us? We couldn't bend over or walk right or even sit! You know what that would look like!"

"No," she said. "What?"

"You don't have any imagination at all," I said. "Think hard. I am not going to go around looking like that all day."

"So what are you going to do?" she asked.

"Just hang around here, I guess," I said.

There was a pause and then Elizabeth said, "And wait for your dad to see the horse's haircut?"

"It doesn't look so bad," I said. "I fluffed up the mane before."

Elizabeth didn't answer.

"Do you think he'll notice?" I asked.

For another minute, Elizabeth still didn't answer. And then she said, "Truthfully?"

"Never mind," I said.

"He'll notice," Elizabeth said.

"I told you, 'Never mind!' " I said. "You were supposed to lie to me. That's what friends do."

"Alex!" Elizabeth yelled. "You're being mean!"

"I'm sorry," I said. "I'm just having a bad day. Things are really messed up." I lowered my voice. "Dad's going to be furious if he notices about the rocking horse. I mean, furious. Why didn't I just leave it alone? And yesterday I almost killed Meg with those stupid cats, and last night we got caught by Mrs. Thatcher. If Mom and Dad find out about that, that we left the house and were running around outside in the dark, I'm dead. There will go our whole deal."

I didn't add one other part — something I was beginning to think about a lot. I was beginning to think that I didn't just want to get this A for Mom and Dad, or even just for baby-sitting. I wanted to *feel* grown-up, too, maybe even that word that Mr. Griffin kept using — responsible. It just felt so good when I remembered to do something right, like when I turned in my book report on time this week, or when I saw that Meg was beginning to wheeze the other day when we were playing and I made her stop and rest. I *felt* grown-up at those times. And it felt good.

Yet things kept happening to mess me up.

"So come to the mall with me, you'll feel better," Elizabeth said. "Melinda calls it retail therapy. Maybe I can get her to take us, or my mom will. I'll tell Mom I have to buy school supplies or something. Listen, I have an idea — we could put the eggs in our backpacks!"

But nobody wears backpacks to the mall on Saturday. Backpacks are for school. But if it was a choice of that or carrying them in our pockets or a —

"Wait a minute!" I said. "I have an idea. We could put them in shopping bags or little store bags. You know, like if you have to return something you bought to a store, how you bring it back in a bag? We could just put the eggs in store bags. Nobody would know!"

"Right!" Elizabeth said. "I'll get a bag and you get one. I'll call you after I find out if my mom will take us. See you!"

"Wait!" I said. "Elizabeth? If you're right about the horse, maybe . . . maybe I better be somewhere else when Dad finds it. Could I stay over your house tonight?"

"Sure!" Elizabeth said. "I'll ask my mom."

I had just settled back on the couch when the phone rang again. Again! What was this — lie down, and make the phone ring?

I leapt to my feet — remembered just in time — and grabbed my egg.

I picked up the phone, still egg juggling.

I already *hated* this egg!

It was Elizabeth, saying her sister Susan was driving and they'd be there in a half hour.

I raced upstairs to ask Mom if I could go and she said yes.

Usually, Mom hates malls. She doesn't think I should be just hanging out there — mall cruising, she calls it. But I told her what Elizabeth had just said — that I needed some school supplies.

I didn't know if she'd let me stay at Elizabeth's. She usually doesn't let me do two nights in a row away. So I decided I'd just call later, from Elizabeth's.

Downstairs in the recycle bin, I found a small bag from the earring store at the mall, and put my egg in it. Then I put that bag inside another bag, one with a little handle attached.

I slung that over my wrist, then went about putting some stuff in my pockets — my wallet, some money, my comb and keys. And then I went downstairs just as Elizabeth and her sister drove up.

It was Susan who was driving us, and she had her friend Denny along, and they had the radio on so loud that even if Elizabeth and I wanted to talk in front of them, we couldn't hear ourselves.

Usually I like the radio, but I was glad when we finally got to the mall. The noise was practically deafening.

Susan and Denny said they'd meet us at three o'clock, and they went their way and we went ours.

"Where to?" Elizabeth said as soon as they were gone. "Aren't you glad to be here? I mean, I can't believe how bored I was last night, how can anyone be as snobby as Robin and her friends but some of the girls are okay, like — " And then she stopped short, actually interrupting herself.

"Look at that!" she said.

She was looking in the window of the earring store, where there was a display of huge earrings. Both of us love earrings, but Elizabeth really loves the huge ones. These looked almost like saucers.

Boy! I couldn't wait till I could have my ears done. But I didn't want the kind of earrings Elizabeth liked. I had already picked out my first pair — double hearts, pink with tiny pearls inside them.

We both leaned close to the window, and as I did, the bag on my arm swung forward.

I heard the sound. A soft, sort of a squishing sound. Followed by a *crack.*

I looked at Elizabeth to see if she'd heard, too. But she was intently twisting her head this way and that, trying to see the price tags that were hidden under the earrings. She didn't seem to have heard.

My egg! It was broken, I knew it.

I was afraid to look. But slowly, I opened the bag and fished out the egg.

It seemed all right. Not ooozy or crushed. But when I turned it over, I could see a tiny crack running all the way from the top to the bottom, no wider than a hair. Soon it would be bigger, wider, though. And then what? I was on my honor to tell if I broke my egg and had to start over.

"You'll be all right, egg," I said softly. "The crack won't get worse, I promise."

"What'd you say?" Elizabeth said, turning to me.

I slid the egg back into the bag. What was I — weird — talking to an egg?

"Nothing," I said, and I turned away.

And that's when I saw it.

"Elizabeth!" I said. I grabbed her arm, turning her with me. "Look!"

"What?" she said.

"That!" I said, pointing.

The pet store! The mall pet store! The solution to our problem.

But Elizabeth was shaking her head. "You are weird!" she said. "Weird, weird, weird, I mean it. After all that trouble you got into with the cats! You must be weird! I can't believe you're even *thinking* cats again!"

"I'm not thinking cats," I said. "Definitely not thinking cats. But I'm thinking something. How much money do you have?"

"Money?" she asked.

"Money," I answered.

She turned back to look in the window of the earring store. She sighed.

"Some," she said sadly.

"Enough for a hamster?" I asked. "A gerbil?"

"Meg's allergic!" she said.

"We could keep it at your house," I said. "We could *both* care for it. You don't want to spend all day today and tomorrow with an *egg*, do you?"

Elizabeth shook her head. "No way! You know my mom. *No* pets. N-O Pets. I mean, if you stay over tonight, okay. But you'd have to take it with you tomorrow. My mom would dump it right out in the yard, she did that once when I brought in some frogs, remember? I mean it, she would."

Yeah. I remembered that. But if we couldn't keep it there, maybe I could keep it in my room. In a box. In my closet. Meg *couldn't* be allergic to a gerbil that she couldn't touch or see, one that was hidden deep in my closet.

"Come on," I said to Elizabeth. "We'll get something. I'll keep it at my house. In my closet. I won't even let Meg in my room."

And I began pulling her in the direction of the pet store. To get something. Anything. As long as it was *not* an egg.

Nine

We didn't have enough money for a hamster or a gerbil, so we settled on a mouse, a black one. I would have chosen a white one because the black one looked too much like a real mouse. Well, I guess it *was* a real mouse, but I mean a regular mouse. Elizabeth, though, said the white one was spooky-looking, like the ghost of a mouse, so I went along because she had more than half the money.

But it was expensive to get even a mouse. We needed special, strawlike bedding for it, and special food for it, and we needed a cage! We definitely did not have money for a cage, so we decided to use something else, like a shoe box, and punch holes in the top.

The man at the pet store warned us that that wouldn't work, but I knew it would — if we got a very strong box, like the kind hiking shoes come in. And then the man gave us a little carrying box to take the mouse home in.

The mouse made little peeping sounds all the way home, more like a bird than a mouse. Fortunately, Susan and Denny had the radio on superloud again, so they didn't hear.

But Elizabeth and I were hysterical laughing each time it peeped like that.

As soon as we got to Elizabeth's house, we raced to her room so I could call Mom and ask about sleeping over.

"Another sleepover?" Mom said when I asked. "I don't think so, Alex. I'd like you home. You know I don't like your having sleepovers two nights in a row."

"But, Mom!" I said.

I had to think fast. Maybe Elizabeth could come to my house? Even though I did not want to be home when Dad found the horse, still, maybe if Elizabeth was there, Dad wouldn't be so mad. Or wouldn't act so mad. But anyway, we *had* to share this project — this mouse.

"How about if Elizabeth sleeps over our

house?" I asked. "We have a school project to work on together."

"Honey," Mom said, sighing. "We need quiet around here. Dad woke up this morning with a terrible cold. He's been sick in bed all day, and he'll probably be in bed tomorrow, too."

"Oh, good!" I breathed.

"Excuse me?" Mom said.

"I just said, 'Oh, gosh!' Please, Mom? Elizabeth and I will be really quiet. We won't disturb Dad. It's important, Mom." And then I had a thought — a way to get her to say yes. "We have to work together on this science project, Mom," I said. "You know how hard I'm working to get an A!"

There was a pause, and then Mom sighed. "Okay," she said. "Okay. You may have Elizabeth sleep over. But this is the last time you have sleepovers two nights in a row, right, sweetie?"

"Right. Thanks, Mom!" I said. And I hung up.

Then Elizabeth ran downstairs and asked her mom and her mom said yes, and we packed up some stuff and then we were out of there.

We raced for my house, carrying the mouse

in its carrying case and ran right up to my
room.

When we got up there, I closed and locked
my door.

Then we settled the little mouse into a good-
sized shoe box — a strong one — and lined it
all with the straw bedding, and gave him some
food. We also got a tiny jar lid for him to use
as a water dish.

"He needs a name," Elizabeth said. "How
about Mickey? Mickey the Mouse?"

"Everybody calls a mouse Mickey!" I said,
making a face at her. I stroked the little mouse
with one finger.

His nose twitched.

"How about Archibald?" I said. "He looks like
an Archibald."

"How about Mortimer?" Elizabeth said. "My
sister, she once had a lizard, and it was named
Mortimer, I think, and it was awful, it smelled,
at least that's what Melinda said but Melinda
says *everything* smells. I think that's why Mom
says no pets, not ever anymore. Why Archibald?"

"Why not?" I said. "I like it."

Elizabeth shrugged. "I guess. Anyway, if we

named him Mortimer, he might start to smell.
Archibald." She reached into the box and patted him. "Hi, Archibald," she said softly.

He snuffled at her hand.

"He likes his name," Elizabeth said.

Then, Elizabeth and I each got out our notebooks and began recording stuff about him,
from buying him, to caring for him, naming
him, feeding him, holding him, everything.

He really was awfully cute as he settled into
his little box. He was doing so many funny
things, like making a nest for himself, tearing
up tissues that we put in the box for him, that
by the time Mom called us to dinner, we had
filled up pages and pages of our notebooks.

It sure was a whole lot better than watching
an egg!

Before we went down to dinner, we put the
top on the shoe box, after first punching holes
in it so Archibald could breathe. Then, just to
be sure, I put a shoe on top of the top. Then
we put the box in the closet, closed the closet
door, and closed my room door, too.

There! No way Archibald was going anywhere. And no way Meg could catch allergies
from him.

Elizabeth and I went down to dinner.

Mom and Mark and Meg were already at the table, and Dad was there, too. Dad looked awful, his nose red and his eyes puffy. He kept sneezing and snuffling, and he sounded almost as bad as Meg had the other day.

I looked at Meg. She wasn't at all puffy or snuffly anymore.

"How are my Barbies?" I asked.

Meg smiled. "Ken took them all for a ride in the car today — one at a time."

Mom just rolled her eyes. "Why can't one of the Barbies drive?" she asked.

Mom is very big about girls being able to do everything that boys can do, like be in charge, and she never misses a chance to point that out to Meg and me — even when it's just a dumb game, like now.

"The Barbies can drive," Meg said. "But today was Ken's birthday, so they let him borrow their car."

I had to laugh. Meg has the weirdest — and best — answers. Although, sometimes, I suspect she just makes up ones that she thinks will satisfy Mom — or shush Mom up.

"Where were you today?" Mark asked, turning to me. "I was at the field and your team was practicing. Coach was looking for you and Elizabeth, too. He said you were supposed to be there."

I shrugged. "Long story," I said.

Dad frowned at me. "Alex!" he said. "That's part of our deal. If you have practice you should — " He suddenly grabbed for his handkerchief, sneezed like he was about to blow the top of his head off, then went on, " — be there."

"I know," I said. "But — "

"But we couldn't!" Elizabeth interrupted. "We both meant to go, we wanted to go, we were talking about it on the phone this morning, about how important it is to be responsible, but we had to carry around a raw egg and you know we couldn't play *soccer* when we were carrying an egg. Did Alex tell you about the project? I mean, that's a big responsibility, that egg project, even if it is kind of stupid and then once we got the egg — "

I kicked her.

But she had already stopped short at that exact moment.

Too late.

"That's right!" Mom said. "That's the important project you're working on tonight." She was smiling at me. "So where is the egg now? I thought you had to carry it around with you?"

I looked at Elizabeth and she looked back at me.

"Uh, no!" Elizabeth said suddenly. "We got something else instead, at my house, my sister, you know Melinda, she has this I told you about it, this lizard, Myron, I mean, Mortimer, he's not bad, really, even if he is a lizard and he smells awful and — "

Dad sneezed again, so loud he made everyone jump.

"Excuse me," Dad said, getting up. "I think I should go back to bed. I feel miserable. And no sense giving this cold to everyone else."

"I'm sorry, honey," Mom said. "Do you need anything? Can I bring you up some soup?"

Dad shook his head. "I'll just get a good night's sleep."

He came around the end of the table and bent over Mom, kissing her on the top of her head. "Don't worry," he said. "I promise to be well enough to finish your rocking horse so you can bring it to the office Monday. I'll feel much better in the morning."

"Don't worry about that," Mom said. "Just get better."

Elizabeth and I exchanged looks.

For the first time in my life, I wished that my dad would be sick. Sick. All day.

After Dad left, Mark talked about soccer and Meg talked about school, but, fortunately, Mom seemed to have forgotten about the lizard and the egg.

Then, when dinner was over, Elizabeth and I went to my room and we stayed there most of the rest of the night. Archibald really was a lot of fun to watch. If this really was learning responsibility, it wasn't too bad. And when we got tired of him, we settled into bed to read and talk and then, pretty soon, we both fell asleep. We had been up much of the night at Robin's and we were both tired. But before we went to sleep, we set the alarm because we had to get up at two o'clock in the morning to see if Archibald needed anything. Everyone had to check on their pets — or eggs — at two A.M. *On our honor.*

But it wasn't nearly two o'clock yet when I

was awakened — me and Elizabeth both. The clock on the bedside table said twleve-ten. And something was in our bed. Something was in our bed down at the bottom. Something that was making a weird and snuffling noise.

Ten

"Elizabeth?" I said. "Is that you?"

"Is what me?" she said, sounding very scared. "No, it's not me."

"It's not me, either," I said.

We both sat straight up, listening.

Snuffling. *Loud* snuffling. At the foot of the bed.

I reached down and touched something — something *big* under the covers — and pulled my hand back, terrified.

Not something. Some*one*.

Someone was in bed with us.

"Elizabeth?" I said. "Someone's down there."

I moved over closer to her, and I felt her reach for my hand.

"What?" she whispered, her voice shaking.

"Someone's down there," I repeated.

"I know," she answered. "I mean, I don't know. Who is it?"

We sat there shaking, hanging on to each other's hands.

"Who are you?" I said to the thing at the foot of the bed.

No answer. No sound at all. Even the snuffling had stopped.

"Who is it?" I said louder. "Who are you?"

Still no answer.

"A ghost," Elizabeth said. "A ghost. Or a monster. It *is* a monster!"

"I'm *not* a monster!" a voice said.

Elizabeth and I grabbed each other harder.

But then I said, "Meg? Is that you, Meg?"

"Yes!" she said, and she sounded like she was crying. "It's me. And I'm *not* a monster!"

"Well, come up here!" I said. "What are you doing here anyway?"

Meg scrambled up from the foot of the bed and even in the dark, she seemed to have radar that led her right into my arms and into my lap.

I could feel her little body trembling. I held her tight and rocked her a little.

"What's the matter?" I asked. "What happened?"

"I was scared," she said.

"*You* were scared!" Elizabeth said.

"Yes," Meg said. "There's noises in my room."

"Noises?" I said. "So what? There are always noises at night, little noises."

"It wasn't little noises," she said. "It was big noises."

"Well, why'd you come in here? Why didn't you go to Mom or Daddy?" I asked.

"I did. But Daddy was snoring so Mommy couldn't hear me. So I came to you."

Great.

"Okay," I said. "But everything's okay now. You can go back to bed."

I reached to the table, turned on the bedside light, and then started to get up. "Here," I said, reaching for her hand. "We'll check out the noises and then you can go back to bed.

"No!" Meg said. "I'm not going in there. There's a ghost or a monster there.

"Meg, there's no such thing as ghosts or monsters!" I said.

"Is too," she said. "Elizabeth just said so."

I sighed. "Elizabeth did not say so."

"I did too," Elizabeth said.

"You are *so* annoying!" I said to Elizabeth, and I glared at her.

I turned to Meg then. She was actually shivering, she was so scared.

"All right," I said. "You can stay here. But you have to promise to go right to sleep. And you can't toss around and wiggle. You have to lie perfectly still."

"I will," she said. "I won't wiggle. But I need Raggles."

I sighed. "Okay, go get him."

"You," she said.

"You!" I answered. "You're the one who wants him."

Her lip came out. "No," she said. "There's noises in there."

"I'll get him!" Elizabeth said, and she jumped out of the bed. "I'll be right back."

She was! Fast! She hadn't brought Raggles, either. And she looked as scared as Meg had looked.

"There are *noises* in Meg's room!" she said, and she dove into the bed.

"Told you," Meg said. She didn't sound so scared anymore, though. She sounded kind of pleased.

"What kind of noises?" I said.

"Go listen!" Elizabeth said, pulling the covers up to her chin.

She and Meg huddled close together, both of them looking up at me.

Geez! It was midnight. I was tired! And now it was like I had *two* baby sisters!

I shook my head and went down the hall to Meg's room. But I didn't feel nearly as brave as I was acting to Meg and Elizabeth. I decided not to go into Meg's room. I just stood outside the door, listening.

There *was* a noise in her room. A loud noise, a scratchy, loud noise.

My heart was pounding hard, but I reached inside the door and switched on the overhead light. The noise stopped for a moment, then instantly started up again.

Slowly, I went into the room.

The sound was loudest near the front wall, over by the toy box.

Carefully, on tiptoe, I went over to the toy box, snatching Raggles from Meg's bed on my way. Yes. The noise was definitely coming from the toy box.

The toy box? How could a toy box be making noise?

Cautiously, *very* cautiously, I opened the box, then jumped back.

Nothing. Nothing was moving. I couldn't see a thing that was making a noise. But the noise was defnitely in there. And suddenly, I was so relieved I almost laughed out loud. I thought I knew exactly what it was — one of Meg's windup toys had unwound, had sprung its spring and was spinning around in there, round and round and round.

That's all it was.

I bent over the toy box and began lifting out toys.

The whirling, scratching sound went on beneath me.

I dug deeper in the box. I took out Meg's beat-up yellow lion, Gruffy, with the stuffing now coming out between his ears. I lifted out a bent, cardboard suitcase filled with Corgi cars. Then a pink plastic car without any wheels. Under them, I scooped out a handful of Legos. Then a plastic doll without any clothes and without a head — and I almost had a heart attack right on the spot.

Because as I moved aside the headless doll, something jumped out at me.

Jumped out.

A mouse. It leapt out of the box, ran right across my feet, and sped across the room, heading for the door.

A black mouse. *Our* mouse?

I ran after him, slamming the door shut.

But he flattened himself. Went under the door. Like a shadow. And was gone.

I raced out in the hall. But there was no light.

I found the light switch and turned it on, praying that Mom and Dad wouldn't wake up.

I looked everywhere, up and down the hall.

Nothing. Not a single mouse in sight.

It couldn't be *our* mouse. It couldn't be.

It was just an ordinary mouse, a regular household mouse.

Please, God, just an ordinary mouse.

I went back to my room, turning out the hall light as I went.

"Did you hear it?" Elizabeth whispered.

"Did you?" Meg said.

I nodded, but I didn't say anything.

I dropped Raggles onto the bed, then went over to my closet. I didn't open the door wide, because I didn't want Meg to see what I was doing in there. But I dug way in the back and reached around till I found the box.

I pulled it forward into the light. And looked in.

In the mouse box. The mouse box with a hole chewed through its side. The *empty* mouse box.

Eleven

There was a mouse loose in the house.

Meg was allergic to anything with fur.

We had wasted eleven dollars and seventy-nine cents buying and outfitting the stupid mouse. Five dollars of that was mine — a quarter of what I needed to have my ears pierced. All wasted!

And we didn't have our pet for the project!

Also, even though it was probably stupid of me, I felt a little sad about the mouse being gone. We had only had Archibald for a few hours, but I had begun to like him — well, whatever. I'm not sure you actually *like* a mouse. And I felt responsible for him. What if something happened to him? What if he stayed lost and starved to death?

Elizabeth and I lay awake a long time whispering, trying to figure out what to do, while beside us Meg curled up on her side and fell sound asleep, Raggles clutched in her arms.

Boy, did I wish I was a little kid again.

After a while, Elizabeth and I fell asleep, too. But we woke early and got up, before anyone else was awake. And we searched the house. First, we looked in the mouse box, hoping against hope that the mouse had just decided to come back, maybe for food. But he hadn't.

We started in the basement and went up, floor by floor. We spent the most time in the kitchen. He'd surely get hungry and go looking for food. And what if he came running out into the kitchen when Mom or Dad were in there? *That* was something to think about!

But even though we looked and looked, no mouse. Nowhere.

Elizabeth had to leave early for church, and when we said so long, neither of us knew what to do. But we agreed to call later and talk about it.

And *I* still had to worry about Dad and the rocking horse.

I went upstairs and would have gone back to bed, but Meg was now sprawled out right in the center, having taken over the entire bed.

She had thrown all the blankets and pillows on the floor, just like always.

Her bed always looks as if a pack of dogs has slept there.

I was just sitting down at my desk, about to see how much change I had in my change jar, when Mark came in.

"What's Meg doing in here?" he said softly, sitting down on the bed, and picking up a blanket from the floor. Very gently, he covered her up.

"She heard noises last night," I said. "She got scared."

"Noises?" he said. "What kind of noises?"

Mouse noises.

I just shrugged.

"Poor Dad," Mark said. "He was sure feeling miserable yesterday. I'm going to finish the rocking horse for him this morning."

"What?" I said.

"I know how to do it," he said. "Dad says it just needs polishing, is all. I thought I'd surprise him and finish it for him."

I started to say, no, don't do that. But then I had a thought — maybe it was better if Mark did it. If the mane looked a little weird, Mark would just think it was supposed to be that way. I mean, real horses, their manes aren't perfectly even, are they? And then, maybe Dad wouldn't even see it before Mom took it to her office! Maybe nothing would happen because of the haircut!

"Sure, why not?" I said. "Hey, Mark? Did Ryan ask you about going to Disney World?"

Mark nodded. "How'd you know about that?"

"Because Robin asked me, too."

"She did? I thought you hated Robin."

"I do."

"You want to go?" Mark asked.

"No way!" I said. "And spend a week with the Popularity Princess and Dragon Lady? So what did you tell Ryan?"

Mark grinned. "I made up a story — said I couldn't go because I have to be in charge here in the afternoons."

"Won't work," I said. "That's why Robin invited me."

He frowned at me.

"If I go, you don't have to be in charge," I explained. "So Robin can get *you*."

Mark blushed. "Geez," he said. "Well, I'm not going — Robin's a little snob. And Ryan — I don't even like him."

He stood up then, after first giving another look at the sleeping Meg. "She scared me the other day," he said softly. "I felt awful about that, about giving her pizza."

I nodded.

Yeah.

"Oh, well," he said. "I won't screw up like that again."

"*You* screw up?" I said. "You're Mr. Perfect!"

"Am not."

Ha! He didn't have a mouse loose in the house!

"Anyway, it wasn't the pizza," I said. "It was cats. She got sick because I let her pet some cats."

"Cats!" he said. "What cats? She's super-allergic to cats!"

"I know," I said. "It was dumb. But I just wanted to tell you that it wasn't your fault."

Mark smiled at me. "Thanks. I think I'll go work on the rocking horse," he said.

But as he started out of the room, I said, "Mark?"

He turned.

"That rocking horse?" I said. "Well, it's not. . . . I mean, when I saw it in the garage yesterday, I noticed Dad didn't do a great job

with . . . I mean, he usually is great at woodworking. But this one is a little weird somehow. I just didn't want you to be surprised. Or
to say anything to Dad and hurt his feelings.
Maybe it was because Dad was getting sick
that it turned out that way."

Mark was frowning at me. "The rocking
horse?" he said. "It's great."

"When did you see it last?" I asked.

He shrugged. "A few days ago. We both
worked on the mane together, Dad and me. I
did all the gluing while Dad held the strip of
leather. What a job, trying to get it straight!"

Right.

I swallowed hard. "Well," I said. "Just
wanted to warn you."

"Okay," he said. "See you."

He went down the stairs and I started down
after him. There was nothing more I could do
about the horse now. I had tried. Anyway,
maybe Mark might just think the mane had
shrunk as it dried.

Shrunk? *Unevenly?*

I shrugged, like I was answering a voice inside.

I told it to shut up.

Anyway, I was starved suddenly, and decided

to get some breakfast. After that, I'd check
again for Archibald.

Mark went through the kitchen ahead of me,
heading for the back door. Just as the noise
started. The scratching noise inside the cabinet next to the sink, where we kept cereal.

"What was that?" Mark asked, stopping and
turning to me.

"What?" I said. I began humming.

"Shush up!" he said. "Listen."

"I don't hear anything," I said.

Not anything but a mouse. And the wild
thudding of my heart.

Thud, boom, went my heart.

Scritch, scratch, scritch, went the mouse.

"That's a mouse!" Mark said. "I bet anything
there's a mouse in here!"

"Not!" I said. "How could it be? Our house
is clean. It's probably just a . . . you know, I
don't know, probably a cricket or something.
They come in the house when it gets cold out."

A definite, louder *scritch*.

He picked up a newspaper from the table and
began rolling it up. "Stand back!" he said, ad-
vancing toward the cabinet, the rolled newspaper held above his head.

"Stop it!" I said. I grabbed his arm, turning him away from the cabinet. "That's cruel! What if it *is* a mouse?"

"I'll kill it," he said.

"You can't!" I said. "That's mean!"

"It's a *mouse!*" he said, as if that explained everything. "A *mouse!*"

"Mice are okay!" I said. "They have to live, too."

"Not in here they don't."

The mouse or whatever it was in the cabinet was making major noise now, like it was eating the cereal, box and all.

"Some mice are nice!" I said. "Think of . . . Ralph!"

"Ralph who?" Mark said, shaking off my hand and heading for the cabinet again.

"Ralph! On the motorcycle. You know."

But obviously, Mark isn't literary. "You want a mouse in your cereal, fine," he said over his shoulder to me. "But I don't want one in mine."

I jumped on him then, actually hanging on his back. "Stop!" I said. "Don't! You can't!"

Then, I practically strangled him, holding onto his neck and pulling him backward. After a brief struggle, I was able to get him off balance and scramble around in front of him. I stood there panting for a minute, then slowly I opened the cabinet door.

Opened the door and saw a box of Cheerios bouncing — the way you see on TV ads when cereal boxes leap around and sing their little good morning songs.

Only this wasn't a TV ad. This was real life. And when I picked up the box and peered inside, I saw the black mouse. Its nose twitching, eyes darting back and forth as it looked up at me. Looked at me and nibbled at the cereal.

"Is it a mouse?" Mark said softly behind me.

I nodded.

"Give it to me," Mark said. "I'll toss it outside."

I shook my head.

"Alex!" Mark said. "It's a mouse! They're dirty."

"Are not," I said, holding it close to me, then turning to face him. "Not this one."

"How do you know?" he said.

" 'Cause I do."

"It's not Ralph, whoever that is," Mark said.

"How do you know?" I said.

He glared at me. "So what do you think

you're going to do with it?" he said. "You know you can't keep it!"

"Bet?"

"What about Meg?"

"What about her?"

"You know what about her! We were just talking about her, about her allergies."

Right. But I needed an A on this project. School *and* home, Mom and Dad had said.

"I won't let her near it," I said.

"You can't keep it," he said. "I'll tell Mom."

"So tell."

"I will," he said, and he started for the stairs. "I mean it."

At the foot of the stairs, he turned and looked at me. "It's not like it's a *pet,* for Pete's sake," he said.

I could see he really intended to tell Mom.

So I had to say it. "Want to bet?" I said. "Want to bet?"

Twelve

So maybe Mark isn't perfect.

He was so mad he said some words then that I didn't think he knew. And then, for some reason, it seemed to make him even madder when I called Archibald, Archibald, like naming a pet made *having* it even worse.

But after I explained that this was that science project, part of the deal with Mom and Dad, and how I was going to give the mouse away after today; and after I practically swore in blood that I would keep the mouse in my closet — *locked* in my closet, in a *jar* in my closet so it wouldn't get away and get near Meg — then, finally, Mark agreed not to tell Mom and Dad.

But what a pain! You'd think he was Meg's father. He actually made me promise, out loud, that Archibald would be out of the house by tomorrow morning.

"Cross my heart and hope to die," I said.

"You will die, too, if you don't keep your promise," he answered. " 'Cause I'll kill you."

I just made a face at him, but I couldn't do much else. After all, if he told, *I* was dead. And all I had to do was get through this day.

Mark just huffed but he went out to the garage, while I got an old pickle jar from the recycle bin, put Archibald in it with a little bit of Cheerios, then put some holes in the top of the jar and screwed the jar top on tightly.

Then I carried it upstairs and put it in the back of my closet and closed the door. But I felt sorry for Archibald, screwed into a jar like that. I mean, it wasn't a terribly little jar, but a pickle jar isn't huge, either. I'd hate to be closed up like that.

I had other worries, too. I was afraid that even with the mouse in the jar, and even with the closet door closed, some of the mouse hair would get out through the holes in the top and get on Meg.

So I tried to wake her up. But Meg is impossible to wake in the mornings. And even though I got her out of my bed, I had to half carry her, and she kept collapsing back against me.

"Come on, Meg!" I said. "Wake up."

But she wouldn't. And then, when I finally did manage to get her pushed out into the hall, she yelled, "Leave me alone, I'm sleeping!" I think she really was sleeping, too. Even when she yelled that, her eyes were closed.

So I quick led her back to my bed and she just collapsed there, sound asleep.

What else could I do? I couldn't risk having Mom and Dad hear and ask what was going on.

To make sure she wouldn't get mouse hair on her, I stuffed a pillow along the crack under my closet door. It wasn't great, but it was the best I could do.

Then I went to my desk and to the science notebook.

I figured it would be honest to say we got up at two o'clock to check on Archibald because we really did. I didn't think we had to tell that he wasn't there.

Imagine a parent waking up to check on their baby and having the baby gone? Worse — imagine finding the baby inside a cereal box in the morning! Some parent *I'd* make!

I looked at my watch.

Nine o'clock. Elizabeth's whole family went to early services, seven o'clock, so she'd be home by now.

I could hear Mom and Dad up in their room now, moving around and talking.

I hoped Dad was still sick.

I picked up the phone and dialed Elizabeth.

"Oh, Alex!" she said. "What happened? Did you find him? I prayed all morning at church, I even promised that if we got Archibald back, I'd never steal — well, I mean borrow — anything of my sisters again if they said I couldn't. I mean, that's a big promise, because Melinda has such neat stuff, well all my sisters do, but Melinda especially. But I could probably get used to just wearing my own clothes for a while, and maybe I could get them to agree — my sisters, I mean, not my clothes — instead of just borrowing stuff when they don't know about it. But then I thought, we'll never get Archibald back. And anyway, you know what? I met Robin and her parents at church and they're going to the horse farm, but just for the afternoon, so I have a plan. If we can't find Archibald, we need *some* pet, so we can steal the cats again, easy this time. They're already in cat boxes. I know because Robin said they're on medication so they put them in those cat boxes so — "

"I found Archibald," I said.

" — they can rest and be quiet and won't be running around and I could bring them over and we'll take them to your room because it would be easy to keep Meg out of your room if we locked — *What*?" she said.

"I found Archibald," I said again.

"Why didn't you *tell* me?" she said. "You *found* him? Really? I can't believe it! Where? Was he in the closet all the time? Is that where he was? I knew he would be, I knew it!"

"Yeah, well you were wrong. He was in the closet all right — the *cereal* closet. And Mark knows."

"Mark? Why did you tell him? Won't he tell your mom and — "

"I didn't tell him. Well, I did, but I had to. Mark was there when it happened. Can you believe it? He was actually *in* the cereal box."

"*Mark*?"

"No, dummy! Archibald."

"Oh."

"Now what?" I said. "Want to come over and finish this project? We still have all today's entries to do. Elizabeth, do you think we'll get an A?"

"Why not?" Elizabeth said. "We've done everything right so far, I mean except for losing Archibald in the night and — "

"Come over as soon as you can," I interrupted her. "We still have eight entries to do today."

"I'll be there as soon as I change," she said. "Is Archibald all right?"

"I think so," I said. "But I think he's sad. He's in a jar."

"That's mean!"

"He can't chew his way out of a jar," I said.

"Oh, right," she said. "Is it a big jar?"

"Actually, no. It's kind of small, not tiny, but it's all I had."

"I'll see if I can find a bigger one," she said.

And then we hung up and I got dressed and brushed my teeth and then went down to breakfast.

Mom was by the sink, making coffee, and she smiled at me when I came into the kitchen.

Dad was there, too, sitting at the table, reading the newspaper.

"Morning, sweetie," Mom said. "Sleep well?"

I shrugged. "Sort of. Not really." I didn't

think I'd say why. If Meg mentioned the noise, I'd make up some story. But chances are Meg would even forget.

"You're not getting a cold, are you?" Dad asked, looking up at me.

I shook my head. "I'm fine. How do you feel?"

Dad smiled. "Better. Much better."

I tilted my head and looked him over. "You don't look too good," I said.

Dad laughed. "Just need a bit of exercise. Woodworking will be just the thing for me."

I shook my head. "I don't think so," I said. "I think you should stay in bed today." I turned to Mom. She's always trying to get Dad to take it easy. "Don't you think Dad should take it easy today, Mom?" I asked.

Mom gave Dad one of those smiles, those looks I can never figure out — like he is just a big adorable baby. "I think he should do whatever he wants today," she said, and she went over and put a hand on his neck.

Dad reached around, found her hand, brought it to his lips, and nuzzled it.

Yuck! And they've been married for a zillion years.

I'm never going to act so dumb.

We sat down to breakfast and just as I was

finishing, Elizabeth appeared on the back porch. I could see her through the window part of the door, see that she was carrying the biggest jar I had ever seen. It was like those supersize mayonnaise jars that they have in the school cafeteria.

I got up and let her in, and she rested the jar on the counter.

"Whew!" she said. "That was heavy. And this big dog, it was a horse almost, it was so big, it kept chasing me and I thought I'd drop it and — "

She stopped and smiled at Mom and Dad. "Hi, Mr. and Mrs. Warner," she said.

" 'Morning, Elizabeth," Dad said. "Cute little jar you have there."

I rolled my eyes. Why do grown-ups think it's funny to say just the opposite of what's so?

But Elizabeth just said, "Well, it's for that science project and it's big enough, actually. I think so anyway." She looked at me. "You think so?" she added.

I wanted to kill her. What'd she want me to say — yeah, it's big enough for a mouse? Honestly!

"You need a jar for the responsibility project?" Dad said. "What for?"

"Oh, nothing, nothing big!" Elizabeth said, wiggling her fingers.

And then she started to giggle, like she had just understood what she had said.

"Wait a minute," Mom said. "I thought you had to care for an egg. But I remember something — did you say something about a — was it a lizard you said last night?"

"Uh, right!" Elizabeth said. "A lizard. Mortimer, my pet lizard."

"Then . . ." Mom was looking very stern. "Then why do you need a jar?"

Elizabeth and I just looked at each other and neither of us spoke.

"Girls?" Mom said. "Why do you need a jar?"

"A jar?" Elizabeth said.

"Right," Mom said. "A jar."

"Oh," Elizabeth said. "This? You mean this jar?"

"Elizabeth!" Mom said. "That. That jar."

"Oh! Oh, well," Elizabeth said. "Well, you know that lizard, Myron, I mean Mortimer, that I was telling you about yesterday? Well, we're going to keep him there and then make this kind of . . . you know, cage, well, I mean like terrarium, for him and then — "

"Stop! Right now!" Mom said. She turned to

me, one hand up like a traffic cop. "You don't have a pet in this house, do you? Do you have a lizard up in your room? Is that why Elizabeth was here last night? You know that anything like that, fur or no fur, you can't have in this house. Meg is allergic to everything! Do you have a lizard in your room? I mean it, Alex Warner, if you have a — "

This time it was me who held up my hand. Mom was sounding just like Elizabeth.

"Mom!" I said. "I do not have a lizard in my room!"

Mom took a deep breath.

"You do not?" she asked.

"I do not," I answered.

She took another slow, deep breath. "Okay," she said. "Okay. You're telling the truth?"

I swallowed. "I'm telling the truth," I said.

I do not have a lizard.

I have a mouse.

"Well, good," Dad said. "But I guess we still don't understand about the jar. You're just going to work on it here? Right?"

"Right!" Elizabeth said. "Like I was telling you, we're just going to make the cage, I mean, the terrarium, you know, terrarium-cage thing here. But Myron, I mean, Mortimer, isn't here.

I swear, that's true! We're just going to work on it here and then take it to my house."

"Right," I said. I turned to Elizabeth. "Come on. Let's get started."

She picked up the jar, and together we raced up the back stairs to my room, where Elizabeth plopped the jar on my bed.

"Close!" Elizabeth muttered. "That was very close. We could have gotten in big trouble."

But that was nothing. Nothing compared to the trouble that was waiting.

Meg, sitting on the floor in my room, the closet door open. The door open and the mouse jar open.

And in her lap . . . in her lap was Archibald.

"Meg!" I shouted. "Meg!"

Mistake.

Meg squealed. Jumped. And Archibald leapt from her lap. Scooted across the room, practically right over my shoe tops. Out the door. Into the hall.

I saw him dart toward the stairs. And that was the last I saw of Archibald.

Thirteen

I wanted to cry. Or scream.

I wanted to shove Meg in the mouse jar head-first. But I didn't. I didn't because Elizabeth was holding me back. Literally.

As soon as I realized the mouse had disappeared completely, I headed for Meg. "I'm going to get you!" I said.

Elizabeth threw her arms around me, practically climbing up on my back.

"Stop!" Elizabeth said. "Stop! Remember, an A at home, too. Baby-sitting! Your ears pierced."

"I don't care!" I said. "Get off me!"

"You do care!" Elizabeth said. "Your ears! Remember what Mr. Griffin says, 'If you can keep your head when all around you are losing

143

theirs,' you know how he's always saying that, and if — "

"I don't care what he says!" I said, finally shaking Elizabeth off me, although she still kept holding my arm. "He never had Meg for a sister!"

"Hush up!" Elizabeth said. "Will you stop? Besides, you can't murder Meg. Your mom and dad will hear."

I glared at Meg, sitting there on the floor. She was looking up at Elizabeth and me and her lip was all trembly like she was about to cry.

She wasn't tricking me into feeling sorry for her, though.

"I didn't do anything," Meg said, and her voice was trembly, too. "I just found this mouse and — "

"*Found* him?" I said. "You lost him!"

"*You* lost him!" she said. "You scared him loose."

She stood up then and started inching toward the door.

But from the way she was moving, I think she knew perfectly well I wasn't letting her out.

"Oh, no, you don't!" I said, getting between her and the door and closing it. "You're staying

right here till I decide what to do with you. I'm
telling Mom you lost my mouse. I am, I swear."

Of course I wouldn't but she didn't have to
know that.

I looked at my watch and then at Elizabeth.

"Okay, now what?" I said. "We'll get a D or
even an F."

It was one of the few times I can remember
that Elizabeth didn't have an instant answer.
She just sat there for a long time, staring at
the floor.

Finally she said, very quietly, "We could just
fill out the report, make up stuff?" She kept
on staring at the floor. "He'd never know."

She was right; he wouldn't know.

"I guess," I said.

She looked up at me.

I looked back.

But then I shook my head. It's not that I'm
perfect, that I never tell a lie. But it just seemed
wrong.

"But we can't," I said.

Elizabeth nodded. "We can't," she said.

"You should get the cats," Meg said.

Both Elizabeth and I turned and looked at
her.

"They'll catch the mouse for you," Meg said.

And then, suddenly, her lip came out again. "No!" she said, like she had just figured it out. "They'll hurt him."

And then she did start to cry, tears streaming down her face. I swear, she turns tears on and off like a faucet.

I went over and plopped down on the bed. This was just too bizarre!

After a minute, Elizabeth sat down beside me.

And then, a minute later, Meg came over to the bed and sat down, too. But she sat on the other side of Elizabeth.

Meg was hiccuping now, and I saw Elizabeth slide an arm around her.

"There must be something we can do." Elizabeth said. "You know, maybe if we can figure out how to do this, we can make it part of our report and then show how grown-up we were and all, maybe more than anybody else even, but we need to figure out how."

"Yeah," I said. "And how do we figure *that* out?

"Mark," Meg whispered.

"What?" I said.

Meg scrubbed her eyes with her fists.

"Mark!" she said. "Ask Mark. He'll know. He's re . . . rees . . ." She hiccuped.

"Responsible," Elizabeth said.

Right. Ask Mr. Responsibility.

But then I thought — maybe Meg was right — not that we should actually ask Mark, but maybe I should ask myself: What would Mark do?

Right away, though, I realized that that didn't help at all. First, I couldn't even begin to imagine myself being Mr. Responsibility. Second, Mark would never have gotten himself into this situation. Besides, he was already mad at me for having the mouse in the first place. He sure wasn't going to come up with ideas for finding it.

Suddenly, Meg took a deep breath and hiccuped at the same time, so hard that I could feel the whole bed jerk.

"Okay, okay, Meg!" I said. "Stop crying. It's okay. We'll find the mouse."

"*Not* okay!" Meg said. She leaned around Elizabeth and peeked at me, holding onto Elizabeth's arm, ready to dart behind her again. "How?" she said.

"I don't know *how*!" I said. "Not yet."

"You're still mad," Meg said.

Brilliant. But I just shrugged. No sense saying anything and make her more upset. Besides, she seemed to have stopped crying, at least for the moment.

"Can I please go now?" she said.

It was so pitiful the way she said it, that for a minute, I was tempted to get up and hold her, hug her. But I fought off the temptation and it passed.

"Okay," I said. "Go."

And then I had a thought: her allergies. She'd have a big allergy attack!

I jumped up from the bed, grabbed her by the shoulders and turned her to me, looking at her closely. Except that she still seemed upset, she looked all right. And I knew from experience, if she was going to have an allergic reaction, she'd have it fast! Still, I was worried.

"Meg," I said. "Do you feel okay?"

She nodded.

"You sure?" I said.

She nodded again, but her lip came out, like she was going to start crying all over again.

"What *is* it?" I asked, exasperated.

"Nothing," she said.

"Then why are you crying again?" I said.

"I'm s . . . s . . . sad!" she said, hiccuping again. "I'm sad about the mouse."

Geez! She was sad! What about me?

"Well, stop crying," I said, "or Mom will hear. Listen . . ."

I knew what I was about to do was probably a mistake, but I . . . I don't know. I needed to do it. "If we find the mouse, Meg," I said slowly. "And if you're not allergic to it . . . when we're finished with our project, I'll ask Mom if you can have it."

"Me! You'll let *me* have it?" She stared at me, her eyes so round and wide they were like the eyes on those toy dolls I used to have when I was little. "My own pet?" she said. "Promise?"

"No, I don't promise!" I said. "I just promise I'll ask Mom. I don't promise what she'll say."

"She'll say yes. I know she will. Thanks, thanks, Alex!" Meg said. She threw her arms around my neck and hugged me fiercely. "I knew you wouldn't stay mad!" she whispered.

And she raced out of my room and down the hall.

I got up and closed the door and went back and sat on the bed.

"Okay," Elizabeth said, right away. "I've been thinking, I've been figuring this all out.

We have problems but we can work them out. First problem, the allergies, but Meg seems all right, doesn't she? She doesn't look like she's having any allergies, right? Then, second problem, where's our mouse? and then third problem, how to get our mouse back? and then fourth, what if he's a stupid mouse — and what if he's so stupid he runs out in front of your mom and dad, like what if he goes back to the cereal closet — and your mom and dad are still there in the kitchen? And fifth problem, or is this sixth? the biggest problem, what if he doesn't go back there in the cereal box? What if he hides in the attic or something? What if we can't find him? *Soon?* Like in the next hour, we just have today and we're only halfway through and we decided we're not going to lie and make up stuff. And if we don't get that A, everything is messed up, like you can forget baby-sitting, and you know the chances of us finding the mouse soon are like nothing." She stopped. Took a deep breath. And then she said, "Let's get the cats."

I stared at her. "Cats! Are you nuts?"

She nodded. "Think about it! I mean, not so they can catch the mouse, but so we can take care of them. We just put them here in this room, and we lock the door so Meg can't get in or get allergies, then we keep them till this afternoon. I told you they're already in cat boxes." She grinned at me. And then said slowly, "A guaranteed A!"

"Meg will get sick!" I said. "Robin will catch us. And those cats are bad news!"

"How can Meg get sick if we keep them in here with the door locked? And I told you Robin was going to the horse farm for the afternoon."

I shook my head. "Sorry," I said. "No way."

Elizabeth folded her arms. "Okay, genius," she said. "So what's your plan?"

I shrugged. "I'll think of one."

Elizabeth just stared at me. For a long time she just stared and for once in her life she didn't say anything.

"Archibald might come back," I said.

"Right," Elizabeth said, and she looked at her watch.

I looked at mine, too. Geez, we were in trouble if we couldn't get Archibald soon. Stupid mouse!

Elizabeth just sat down on the bed. "Well, I guess we just wait, and it's getting later and later, and we're only halfway through, but that's all right because Archibald *might* come and — "

"All right, all right!" I said. "Do it."

"*Do* it?" she repeated.

I nodded. "Do it. We go get the cats."

It was berserk and bizarre. It was more dangerous than anything we had done so far. But Elizabeth had a plan and I had none. And it was desperation time.

Fourteen

This was the most dangerous part of our project, yet for some weird reason, it turned out to be the easiest to do.

First, when we got to Robin's, the two cats were already in two cat cages, with carrying handles attached, just like Elizabeth had said they would be. Besides all that, they were both sleeping and quiet as anything. Maybe the medicine that they were getting for their upset stomachs made them sleepy. I don't know. All I know is, they didn't make a sound.

We each picked up a cage and walked right out of Robin's garage — out the front door. No need to sneak out back and climb over the fence, since we knew nobody was in the house to see us. Also, in case some neighbor saw us, we had decided to act really cool about this, say that we were supposed to be caring for the cats. But we knew we would have to be very careful when we got near my house.

When we got there, I handed Elizabeth my cage and she waited while I ran around the corner and checked things out.

I snuck around the side of the house, up to the back door, and peeked into the kitchen.

Perfect. Nobody around — not in the kitchen, the yard, anywhere. That meant the coast was perfectly clear. Thank goodness for the back stairs that go up from the kitchen.

I went back to Elizabeth, picked up my cat, and then, cool as anything, we walked right up to the house and in the back door.

Nobody around, no one at all. Of course, for a second, I realized that was both good and bad — it could mean that Dad was out in the garage. But maybe not, and anyway, he might not even notice the horse's haircut.

We were heading for success at least. An A in the science project. An A at home, what with Meg so happy with my Barbies and TV and all. And I hadn't gotten her in trouble even once in the past week.

Baby-sitting. Money. My ears pierced.

Very quietly, Elizabeth and I went up the

stairs. At the top, I took one more quick look around out into the hallway.

Nobody, not even Meg.

Elizabeth and I tiptoed across the hall to my room, then went in and shut the door behind us.

"We did it, we did it!" Elizabeth said, putting her cat cage down on the bed and turning to me. "I can't believe we did it, but I knew we could, I just knew it, didn't you?"

"No," I said.

"No?" she said. "How come?"

I just shook my head at her. "How come? Because we could have gotten caught, because Mom could have seen us, or Robin could have come home, or the cats could have — "

"You worry too much," she interrupted. "Come on, let's let them out."

I put my cat cage down next to hers on the bed.

Both cats were still awfully quiet, although they were both awake — staring at us through the mesh openings. One of them, the one right in front of me, was all puffed up, its fur sticking out every which way. It wasn't nice fluff, either, you could tell; it was mad fluff, like that Halloween-cat look it had had the other day.

Its mouth was pulled back in that same mad grin, too, just like then.

I started to go behind Elizabeth so I'd get around the other side, be in front of the tame-looking cat.

But Elizabeth isn't as dumb as Meg.

"I call this one!" she said, reaching for the unfluffed cat. "You get that!"

She was already unlatching the cage of the quiet cat.

She lifted him up gently, and set him on the bed.

He turned around, sniffed at the blanket, then sniffed at Elizabeth's hand.

"You're a good kitty, aren't you?" she said to him softly. "A nice kitty."

She turned to me. "Let yours out. We have to hold them, you know and pat them, and everything. Where's your notebook? We have to record everything, isn't this fun? It beats the egg, doesn't it?" She looked up at me and giggled then. "Did you hear that?" she said. "I said, 'It beats the egg,' but I didn't mean it that way, like egg beating, you know? You know what, I just thought of something, could you ever *eat* an egg again, after being a mother hen, you know carrying it around and all? Do you think that's how a mother chicken feels, protective of her egg? Weird, huh?"

"What's weird is you have the good cat," I said. "I have the bad one. Again."

I was taking my time about letting my cat out of its box. No way was I going to lift it out and get scratched to death. I just opened the box and hoped the cat would climb out by itself.

"Uh-oh!" Elizabeth said suddenly. "Now what are we going to do?" She had gone to the desk and picked up her notebook.

"What?" I said, still eyeing the mean-looking cat. It had climbed out and was standing on the bed now, but it was all hunkered down, like it was about to pounce.

Elizabeth waved the notebook. "This!" she said. "All the entries yesterday are about the *mouse*. We've got cats now!"

"No problem," I said.

"No problem?" Elizabeth wailed. "We said we weren't going to lie!"

"It's not a lie!" I said. "We did care for a pet — we just changed the kind of pet. So wherever we have the word *mouse*, we just put *cat*."

"A cat in a *shoe* box?" Elizabeth said.

I shrugged. "So we don't call it a shoe box," I said. "We call it a . . . cat box!"

"With straw bedding and a baby-food jar lid for water?" Elizabeth said doubtfully.

"Details, details." I grinned at her. "You worry too much," I said, mimicking her. "Anyway, what matters is we have a pet. We're caring for it, holding it, recording our feelings about it. That's all that counts."

"Isn't," Elizabeth said, very sad sounding. "We're on our honor. You know Mr. Griffin made a big deal of that."

I was — am — as honest as Elizabeth is. But no way was I letting her spoil this. We had come a long way and risked a lot for this. And this wasn't the kind of lie like in making up fake entries. This was just a *change* of pets.

I put my hands on my hips and glared at her. "On our honor to care for a pet," I said. "On our honor to get up at two A.M. and record what it's doing. On our honor to record our feelings and tell if we broke the egg. He didn't say anything at all about 'on our honor' not to change pets in the middle. You know he didn't say anything about that at all."

And he hadn't. He had probably never thought of it.

"You sure?" Elizabeth said.

"Of course, I'm sure," I said. "Besides, I bet anything Robin is doing the same thing, or else she's going to totally lie. If she was caring for her cats Saturday and Sunday, she'd be here right now. I bet she switched from cats to horses. Now come on, what's our first observation today?"

I picked up my own notebook and looked over at my cat.

"That your cat is mad!" Elizabeth said.

"And yours is purring," I said, bending over and listening to her cat, which was now curled up on the bed.

"That's because I'm a better mother than you are," Elizabeth said smugly.

But I knew she was just joking.

And that's the last sensible thought I had for a long while. Because at that precise moment, all these things happened — *at the same exact moment:*

A mouse came scurrying under the crack in the door.

Both cats leapt from the bed.

Pounced.

Elizabeth and I dove for them.

We both screamed.

My door burst open.

Meg raced in, barefoot, wearing just underpants and her pajama top, screaming, "My mouse, I found my mouse!" at the top of her lungs.

From downstairs, I could hear Mom and Dad both yelling — Dad hollering something about "the rocking horse," and Mom yelling something that sounded a lot like, "Alexandra, get down here this minute!"

The mouse turned and raced for the closet, both cats in pursuit, knocking Meg over as they raced between her legs.

And as Meg tumbled and fell against the bed, the huge mayonnaise jar that had been on the bed went crashing to the floor, splitting into a million jagged pieces.

I have never moved so fast in my whole entire life.

I leapt across the room in two huge strides, and swept Meg up off her feet and into my arms.

She immediately began to scream, adding her voice to the din in the house. "Stop it! Put me down, put me down! I need to find my mouse."

She was kicking fiercely at my shins.

But no way was I putting her down. She was barefoot and there were zillions of tiny shards of glass all over my floor, all over my rug.

And wait'll Mom got a load of that!

Which was just about to happen.

When I carried Meg out into the hall, Mom and Dad were both racing up the stairs. I still had Meg in my arms, and could see them coming up, Dad taking the steps two at a time, wide-eyed, scared-looking.

Scared and then more scared, as both he and Mom were almost bowled over by the cats, who had now escaped from my room and were racing down the stairs, running faster than I could have thought possible.

In pursuit of a small, black mouse.

It was all over now. All over but the trouble.

Forget the A.

Forget the baby-sitting.

Irresponsible.

Carefully, I set Meg down, and as soon as she was loose, she ran, too — down the steps, past Mom and Dad, after the two cats and the mouse.

I turned.

Elizabeth was right behind me in the hall, plastered back against the wall, like she was trying to shrink out of sight.

She grabbed at my shirt, clutching the bottom hem.

"Ohmigosh, ohmigosh, ohmigosharewein-trouble!" she whispered.

The understatement of the year.

Fifteen

There was an instant of eerie quiet.

And then Mom said, "What was that I just saw?"

She and Dad were standing in front of me and Elizabeth, staring at us.

Neither Elizabeth nor I answered.

"Tell me that was not a cat, two cats," Mom said. "Tell me that was not a cat I saw just now."

For just an instant — half an instant — I was tempted to say, "Okay, that was not a cat you saw just now."

But I was smart enough not to.

"Answer me," Mom said.

"It's, uh, yes," I said.

"Yes? Yes, what?" Dad roared.

He really did roar.

163

Elizabeth was still holding onto my shirt, and she backed up even further, taking me with her, like she was trying to make us part of the wallpaper.

"Yes, Mom, yes, Dad," I said.

"That's not what I meant!" Dad yelled. "I meant, yes what? Yes, it was a cat? Yes, it was two cats? How many cats are in here? And where in blazes did you get cats to begin with? And was there a mouse, too? Did I actually *see* a mouse?"

"Hush now, dear," Mom said, turning to him. "Now hush." She put a hand on his arm.

"Don't you hush me!" Dad yelled, and I almost smiled.

I love it when this happens. They get mad at each other for yelling and forget about me. It doesn't happen often, but when it does, I love it.

No such luck this time.

Dad shook off Mom's hand and turned to me. "So what's going on?" he said. "And it better be good. Because, besides these . . . these *cats* . . . you had someting to do with my rocking horse, didn't you? What in *heaven's* name possessed you to do such a — "

Just then Elizabeth yelped and a mouse —

and a cat — came into view, tearing up the stairs and back into my room. Pursued — again — by Meg, screaming at the top of her lungs.

"Stop it!" she yelled. "Stop it, you stupid, mean, stinking cat!"

"Meg!" Mom said, and she reached for Meg. But Meg darted under Mom's arms and headed for my room.

But I was quicker than Mom. I immediately leapt after Meg, and I grabbed her around the waist, lifting her right off the floor.

"No!" I yelled. "You can't go in there!"

"Why not?" Dad said. "What else do you have to cause trouble in there?

He stepped into my room, just as the mouse and cat came racing back out and down the front stairs.

Over Meg's yowling, all we could hear were Dad's footsteps — crunch, crunch; crunch, crunch.

In a minute, Dad appeared back at my bedroom door. He leaned against the door frame.

He was pale and quiet, like all the mad had gone right out of him.

He rubbed one hand across his forehead and just looked at me as I still held Meg, squirming, kicking her bare feet hard against my shins.

Bare feet hurt!

I wanted to yell, "Quit it!" and shake her. But of course, I didn't. I was in enough trouble. So I just set her down, but I still held her firmly around the waist.

"You can't go in there, Meg," I said. "There's broken glass all over."

"Broken glass!" Mom said, and now her voice began rising. "What did you break? What other kinds of trouble are you in now? I can't *understand* — "

"Hush, dear," Dad said to her quietly.

She whirled on Dad, madlike.

But then both of them smiled, just a little, but it definitely was a smile.

Good! I almost sighed with relief, except that at that moment, they both turned back to me. And it was clear that their smiles were for each other only.

I let go of Meg then, and she ran down the front stairs after the cats, just as Mark began calling me from the foot of the back stairs. "Alex?" he yelled. "Come here for a second."

Elizabeth and I looked at one another.

"Alex?" Mark called again. "I have something of yours, I think. Come here."

The mouse?

I looked at Mom and Dad. No way was I going anywhere, I could tell. "Can't," I called back.

I heard Mark start up the back steps. The stairs curve, and as he came into view, I could see his hands were cupped and he held them close against his chest.

"Where're Mom and Dad?" he asked softly.

From where he was, he couldn't see them around the curve, I knew.

I started to say, "Right here," but before I could open my mouth, he went on. "I found a mouse!" he said. "Is it yours? Did it get away again? I don't see how it could if you really put it in that jar. Or is it another mouse, do you think?"

I saw Mom press both hands against her temples, the way she does sometimes like she's trying to keep her head from splitting apart.

I know I should have warned Mark about what he was walking into. But it was too late.

He arrived on the landing, turned the corner into the hall — and came face to face with all of us. Mom and Dad. Elizabeth and me. And Meg, who had reappeared up the front stairs and was crying again.

For a moment, Mark made motions like he

was going to try hiding his hands behind his back. But then he just gave it up and said, "What . . . what . . . happened?"

"Good question," Dad said, wiping a hand across his forehead. "Maybe you can tell us."

Mark just shook his head.

Dad turned to me then. "Maybe *you* can tell us," he said.

I shook my head, too. What could I say?

"I mean it," Dad said quietly, looking right at me. He didn't sound mad. He didn't sound upset. He just sounded weary, puzzled. "I really mean it," he said. "Alex, is there an explanation? Can you tell us what this is all about?"

I looked at Elizabeth and she at me.

We both shrugged.

"Alex?" Dad said again. "I'm asking you a question."

I sighed, then took a deep breath. "It's our responsibility project," I said quietly. "We're learning to be grown-up."

And the weird thing was that nobody laughed.

Sixteen

"Then *be* grown-up," Dad said. "We'll talk after you've cleaned up this mess."

"Meg? Mark?" Mom said. "Come downstairs with us. Let Alex take care of this now."

All of them went down the front stairs, Meg looking at me over her shoulder, Mark first carefully transferring Archibald into my hands.

Leaving me and Elizabeth to try and clean up the mess.

It didn't take long to transfer Archibald to the pickle jar.

It didn't take all that long for us to capture the cats and get them back into their boxes. It didn't take long to get them returned to their garage. But it took forever to clean up all the glass slivers in my room, forever to pick the

169

zillions of slivers out of the rug. But that was nothing compared to how long it took to per-suade Mom and Dad not to get rid of the mouse completely, immediately. Mom even wanted me to set it loose out in the backyard. But Meg immediately set up such a howling that Mom said, "Okay, okay! We'll talk about it later." And they let me leave it in the jar in my closet for safekeeping. "For *now*," Mom kept saying. "Just for now."

I think one reason Mom said that was to keep Meg from getting more upset. Mom and Dad were watching Meg like hawks, waiting for an allergic reaction to show up.

When Elizabeth and I finally had things sort of back to normal, the cats returned and the room cleaned up, Dad called a family confer-ence around the kitchen table.

Elizabeth was invited to join, but she sud-denly remembered she had work to do at home. I knew what she was really going to do, though. She had told me when we were on our way to Robin's with the cats in their cages: *She* was going to stay there in Robin's garage with the cats for the next eight hours to finish the proj-ect, to make her hourly records in the note-book. Eight hours or until Robin came home, whichever came first. She even offered to take my notebook, and to record stuff for me. But I said no thanks. I was failing this project anyway.

And I felt totally miserable. Just miserable. Even worse than I thought I would, and it wasn't just because of not getting an A and baby-sitting and all. It was something else that I had trouble explaining even to myself, but I knew how it made me feel — miserable. It was that something I felt the other day, that I wanted to *be* responsible, grown-up. Some grown-up I was!

It was too late to do anything about it now, though. I had messed up, big time.

After Elizabeth left, when we were all gathered around the kitchen table — Mom and Dad, Meg and Mark and me — Dad began. "Okay, Alex," he said. "Tell us what's been going on."

Before I could even begin, though, Meg went over and climbed into Dad's lap.

I knew why. She was thinking: accessory. She wanted to get on Dad's good side.

It didn't matter to me. I was in so much trouble, there was no way I could be on anybody's good side.

So I began. I told them everything — from the start of the science project, through the first catnapping, the egg problem, the mouse buying, the first mouse escape during the night, the second mouse escape and second catnapping — everything.

I thought of skipping the part about Meg's allergic reaction being my fault since Mark had already confessed to that. But I decided to tell everything. No sense letting Mr. Responsibility take the blame for me, especially since he was in some trouble, too, for not telling about the mouse when he had first seen it.

I told everything. Once, when I got to the part about the mouse in the toy box and Meg in my bed in the middle of the night, I thought I saw Mom and Dad exchange a look, like they were trying not to laugh. But it was just a quick look, and when they turned back to me, they both seemed very mad still, so it was probably just wishful thinking on my part.

Anyway, I told them every single thing, including the part about the horse's haircut and why. But I deliberately left out Meg's role as lookout in the first catnapping.

And then, just as I finished telling the whole

thing, suddenly, I felt like I was going to cry.
I fought it back but I could feel it welling up.
I never cry. I hate to cry! But I couldn't help
it — I was crying.

I knew exactly why, too. It wasn't just failure.
It wasn't about not getting my ears pierced. It
wasn't even about baby-sitting. All of that was
important, but it wasn't the reason I was
crying.

I was crying because I'm a jerk. Because I'll
never grow up.

I began crying hard and couldn't stop. I was
practically sobbing.

Everybody else got real quiet.

Meg came over to me then and tried climbing
into my lap, but I pushed her away.

I didn't want Meg.

I just wanted to go up to my room and get
into bed and hug a stuffed animal and cry myself to sleep.

And to have Mom and Dad bring me hot milk
and soup and tell me what a wonderful child
I am.

Except of course, I'm not.

And then Dad got up and came around the
table. He lifted me up in his arms like I was

Meg's size. Then he went around the table with me in his arms and sat down again, holding me on his lap.

I'm much too big to sit on Dad's lap, to sit on anyone's lap. But I didn't try to get away.

Dad began rocking me, holding me close to him. "Hush now," he kept saying. "Hush, hush, it's all right."

It wasn't all right. But I let him rock me. I put my head against his chest, felt the rough wool of his shirt, smelled his smell of wood shavings and soap — and cried my eyes out. And all the while, he kept saying, "It's all right, you're all right."

And then, over my own crying, suddenly I could hear Meg crying, too, and then Mom began trying to hush her.

This always happens! It makes me so mad. I hardly ever cry, but whenever I do, Meg cries, too. But hers wasn't quiet crying. She was almost hysterical, and then Mom and Mark both were trying to quiet her.

Finally, I couldn't stand listening to her anymore, so I sat up, wiping my eyes with my hands.

"It's okay, Meg," I said. "It's all right. I'm not crying anymore."

But Meg kept right on crying.

"Meg!" I said. "Hush up! It's okay."

Meg kept her head bent. After a minute, though, she took a deep shaky breath and looked up at me, her face streaked with tears.

"Stop it!" I said. "What are you crying for anyway?"

" 'Cause I'm sad," she said. " 'Cause you're sad."

"Well, I'm not sad anymore," I said. "So stop."

"You *were* sad," she said.

I shrugged.

" 'Cause of that deal that Mom and Dad said — about getting an A?"

"No," I said, and like a jerk, I could feel my own tears coming back again, but I fought them down. "No," I said. "That's not why."

"So, why?" she said. "Mom and Dad aren't that mad, are you, Mom and Dad?"

"Because I'm a jerk!" I said. "Because I'm not grown-up. Because I'm a complete failure at being a grown-up. I can't even be grown-up a little bit of the time!"

"Not true!" Mark said. And he said it at almost exactly the same moment that Mom and Dad said practically the same thing.

"That's not true," Mom said.

"It's not!" Dad said, and he took hold of my chin and turned me so I was facing him. "You kept Meg from getting a serious cut before," Dad said. "Mom and I both noticed it at the time, when you kept her from going in your room, when so many other things were going on . . ."

"Yeah," I said glumly. "Like two stolen cats racing around, cats that I wasn't supposed to have, chasing a mouse that I'm not allowed to have and . . ." I swallowed hard. "And making Meg sick!" I said. I started to cry again.

I think that's the part that had been really bothering me, that I hadn't gotten over since Friday, seeing Meg so sick with that allergy attack.

Dad pulled me close again. "Meg's okay," he said softly. "It's okay. There's no need to cry. And you *are* growing up. You did some very responsible things this morning. So you're not all grown-up yet. That's all right. You're allowed to make mistakes. We all do. That's how we learn."

"Besides," Mark chimed in. "You could have blamed me for Friday, and you didn't. I think that's mature."

Mature? I looked up at him. Me?

"And you're being honest with us," Mom said. "I admire that. A lot."

Meg got off Mom's lap then and came and lay her head against me. "I think you're nice," she said. "You let me sleep in your bed when I was scared and you got me Raggles and you offered to sew him up, and you lent me your TV and Barbie collection and everything."

I could only smile at that. It was true — I had done some nice things for her.

Everybody was quiet for a long time then.

Dad was rocking me quietly, and I put my head against his chest again.

After a bit, Dad handed me his handkerchief, and I blew my nose, then sat up straight.

Mom, Meg, Mark, Dad . . . they were all looking at me, watching me with so much . . . What? Love? Like they cared?

Well, of course they cared! But like — like it was all right with them, everything was all right.

Maybe — maybe it was that *I* was all right with them? Even if I wasn't all grown-up yet?

"You know," Dad said quietly, turning my face so I was looking at him again. "You're allowed to be — you're supposed to be — not all grown-up yet."

"Really?" I said.

"Really," Dad said.

And then, for just an instant I was tempted to say: Does that mean I can baby-sit and have my ears pierced?

But I didn't. Because baby-sitting, pierced ears, an A in both projects — they were important. But nothing like as important as this moment.

Seventeen

I wish I could say that everything was all okay after that, but it wasn't. Not completely, anyway. First, I didn't get an A in the school project, but I didn't get an F either. I got an incomplete.

Also, I wasn't allowed to baby-sit — yet. But Mom and Dad said I was making progress, so I could start by sitting for Meg some more, and not just on Friday afternoons. And they were going to pay me, too! One of the first things I was going to do with my money — after having my ears pierced — was buy that Barbie's dream house. But I was going to buy it for Meg.

I'm too old for a Barbie's dream house. But Meg hadn't stopped talking about my Barbies since I lent them to her. She was trying to figure out how she could get money to buy some of her own. She'd like the dream house, maybe for her birthday. And meanwhile, I might even give her some of my collection. I was really too big to play with it anymore.

But one really good thing did happen after that, a realization that was brand new and important.

It was a week later, a Monday night, and Mom and Dad and Mark were downstairs watching *Monday Night Football.* Meg and I were in her room, playing with Archibald — *her* mouse now. Since Meg had shown no allergy to the mouse, Mom and Dad had let her keep it and they'd bought it a cage and a little race thing and everything, so it was all set up.

Meg and I were playing with it, lying on our backs on the floor, taking turns letting it run up and down over our stomachs.

We had had a big argument over who would get first turn, but I won because I said I had paid for it.

When I passed him back to Meg, she cradled him in both hands, then turned to me. "What are you going to do with your baby-sitting money?" she asked.

"Have my ears pierced," I answered.

"Who'll go with you?" Meg asked.

I shrugged. "I'll find somebody. Not Robin's mom. But maybe one of Elizabeth's sisters."

"Mom'll be mad," Meg said.

"They're *my* ears," I said. "Besides, Mom didn't say I couldn't. She just said she wasn't paying. It's my decision."

"Mom's in charge," Meg said.

"Not of *my* ears," I said.

Meg lay back on the floor and set Archibald on her stomach. She was quiet for a minute, then turned her head so she was looking at me. "Who's in charge of my ears?" she asked.

"You!" I said, laughing. "But you don't want to get your ears pierced yet, do you?"

She shook her head. "No," she said. "I was just wondering." She was quiet for a minute, and then she said, "Everybody bosses me around."

I reached over and mussed up her hair. "You're still little," I said. "So you get bossed around some."

"A lot!" she said.

"Well, so do I," I said.

And then suddenly I realized something, something I wasn't exactly sure how to put into words, even for myself. But it had something to do with what Meg had just said.

Maybe, I thought, trying the words out in my head, maybe that's what growing up meant — being in charge, bossing yourself? Maybe it didn't have much to do with baby-sitting cats or carrying an egg around all day. Maybe being grown-up and responsible meant being a *good* boss of yourself!

Meg sighed. "Know what?" she said. "I wish I was grown-up. Like you."

Like me?

I smiled. "Soon, Meg," I said, "soon." I snuggled close to her and hugged her, Archibald and all. "You'll be all grown-up soon. We both will be."